Black Fox Literary

M A G A Z I N E

Issue 24 Cover Art: *Birch Forest* by Karen Boissonneault-Gauthier

ISBN: 978-1-7336240-1-5

Editors' Note

Welcome to Issue 24!

Even with the extra six weeks from the groundhog, we just couldn't get our issue together in time for winter this year. We hope you'll enjoy this year's Spring Issue, though! There were hard decisions to make for this issue, but we did it! The pages are filled with a diverse group of authors, including a graduate from the alma mater of the founding editors. From New York to LA, publishing poetry to children's books, from Pushcart nominees to Grammy nominees, we've put them all in!

This new year is bringing some changes to *Black Fox*. We look forward to sharing them with you, so please keep an eye out for updates on our socials.

We are truly yours,

~ The Editors
Racquel and Elizabeth

Meet the BFLM Staff

Editor:

Racquel Henry is a Trinidadian writer, editor, and writing coach with an MFA from Fairleigh Dickinson University. She is also the Editor-in-Chief at *Voyage YA Journal* and owns the writing studio, Writer's Atelier, in Maitland, FL. Racquel has been a featured author, presenter, and moderator at writing conferences and MFA residencies across the US. She is the author of the novelette, *Holiday on Park, Letter to Santa, Christmas in Cardwick*, and *The Writer's Atelier Little Book of Writing Affirmations*. Her fiction, poetry, and nonfiction have appeared in various literary magazines and anthologies. When she's not working, you can find her watching Hallmark Christmas movies.

Managing Editor:

Elizabeth Sheets is a writer and an editorial associate for the Research Technology Office at Arizona State University. She earned a MA in Narrative Studies from ASU. Some of her favorite authors are Patrick Taylor, Stephen King, Anne Rice, Fredrik Backman, Kristen Arnett, and Sarah Waters. Elizabeth's fiction, nonfiction, and poetry appear in *Kalliope – A Consortium of New Voices, Black Fox Literary Magazine, Mulberry Fork Review,* and *Apeiron Review.*

Reader:

H. Rae Monk is a writer based in Austin, Texas. She was the first graduate from the Narrative Studies MA program at Arizona State University and holds a BA from ASU in English: Creative Writing with a focus on Fiction. Some of her favorite writers are Anthony Horowitz, Joy Harjo, Matt Goldman, Dina Nayeri, Philip Pullman, and J.R.R. Tolkein.

Contents:

Cover Art

Birch Forest by Karen Boissonneault-Gauthier

Winner of the 2023 *Black Fox* "Siblings" Writing Contest

Fiction

Nonfiction

Poetry

Ten Days
By Kay Smith-Blum
Winner of the *Black Fox* "Siblings" Writing Contest

The worst decisions are made in isolation. I let my brother's
ringtone reverberate inside my Volvo. I considered possible
greetings: *I was just thinking about you.* Untrue. Obsess maybe, but
never just thinking. Or *Hey, what's it been? Three years?* True.
Other than one missed call which I didn't return. I've learned not to.
I braked for the crosswalk, eased through the intersection, and
waited through the fourth ring before picking up.

"Cales?"

"I'm FedEx'ing a blood test kit today to you."

My throat caught, just like it had the first time and every
time I had heard his voice. I pulled to the curb. "A little late to
demand proof that we're blood, don't you think?"

"Patrick needs a donor. Cathy and I are getting tested, too."

"A transplant?"

"Stem cell. His leukemia is back."

I clutched the steering wheel. Barb, Patrick's wife, had
called last month. Bryn, their daughter, had an upcoming European
trip with her high school dance troupe. That had been Barb's only
news. "What leukemia?"

"He was diagnosed a year or so ago. Look, they didn't tell
me either until he underwent treatment and went into remission."

Out my car window a large dogwood in the parking strip burst with ivory flowers. The first time I met Cales in person, we had dinner under a dogwood tree in a West Hollywood café courtyard, not that either of us really ate. We couldn't take our eyes off one another, our souls laced together by a familial shoestring, pulled taut and wide awake upon discovery. An electric connection that had proved as problematic as it was magical.

They don't tell you about these things in the adoption-search counseling. They skirt right past the possible pitfalls, but, turns out, this overwhelming surge of emotion is quite common. Finding your blood after a lifetime of no exposure begets a chemical reaction on all sides, akin to a 4th-grader's science exhibit, a bumbling volcano, subject to as many aborts as eruptions.

A therapist had tried to help me sort through it. I said it felt like a teenage infatuation, except not. She had labeled the emotions dormant-primal, like a new mother's need to feel her infant's breath on her cheek. But as daughters find their sperm donor fathers, sons find the unwed teenager who bore them, sisters find the brother they always wanted, the compulsion to experience that contact they have been denied and our society has deemed irrational. The counselor had looked me in the eye. "But, there is a rationale to it. The void created the obsession. Fill the void," she had said, "and it will pass." Two decades later, it had not.

I refocused. "Why isn't Patrick calling me?"

"I told him I would handle it." Raised as the oldest, even though I really am, the imagined control is Cales' drug. He loves emergency mode, ramrodding any disaster into a palatable outcome, forcing those, who would rather not, to act.

After six months of fruitless searching for my birthmother, the agency asked me if I wanted to find my birthfather too. One phone call found my uncle and his wife, Sarah. My birthparents affair had created quite the brew-ha-ha in the Donager family circle, replete with nuns, priests, and cathedral organists. Aunt Sarah gave out numbers for both my birthfather and his oldest son. The searcher called Junior, first, instead of Senior, by mistake. Cales handled it, strong-arming my birthparents into agreeing to contact. *Et, voila!* Three full-blooded Donager siblings and a myriad of aunts, uncles and cousins had materialized.

I checked the time. "Look, I'm late. Folks are waiting for me."

"I'm sure they'll wait."

"You've missed a few beats," I said, unable to resist the dig at his multi-year dearth of communication. "I'm a public official now, elected to the Seattle School Board last year. Constituent duty and all that." I stared at the white blossoms, not sure what to do next, just knowing I could not stay on the call any longer. "I've gotta go."

"So," his voice wavered. "You'll get the test back right away?"

"I'll talk to Patrick."

I hung up and turned the ignition. It grated. The car was still running.

* * *

I sat at my dining room table, running my fingers around the edges of the FedEx box from Baylor Medical Center. My college roommate, Jen, and her doctor-husband, Mike had spent an hour on the phone with me, explaining, among other things, the drugs administered to a donor to pump up their stem cell count before the extraction. Pre-treatment and the transplant would require me to stay in Dallas for ten days. The chill that had rooted inside me during my conversation with Cales had notched up during last night's apologetic call from Barb, the only member of the Donager clan with whom I had thought I had a normal relationship. Then again, this was normal—Donager normal—secrets in every crevasse.

Patrick was back in the hospital undergoing treatment and throwing up a lot. Barb's breath had traveled the line in short, jerky spits. "If you're a match, you can stay with us."

"I'd probably stay with Jen." I phrased my answer as if neither of us knew what would happen. "You've had enough to deal with. Although, I really don't know what." My anger at being kept in the cold had only spiraled in the last 24 hours.

A photo of my real mother, the one who raised me, rested on the dining room nook. Everyone in the South Austin neighborhood of my childhood had brought their problems to her, counting on the fact that she would ask the hard questions, help them find the answers. She had been dead for seven years when I had flown home for another funeral. In a life's-short moment, alone in my hotel room, I had looked for a listing for the Home of the Holy Infancy— you can't make a name like that up—and dialed. Questions still outweighed any answers I had found.

I toted the FedEx box to my clinician. They drew four vials of blood and sent it off. Forty-eight hours later, the transplant coordinator from Baylor hospital called. My siblings had not met the donor criterion. But the one who had been given away was, indeed, a perfect match.

* * *

June in Texas is one long watery wave of heat. It wrapped around me like an unwanted shawl as I exited the airport terminal. My first trip back to Dallas after finding the Donagers, Cathy and her family had picked me up, but she and I had never found our rhythm. I had made a set of the medical records from the Home for my siblings. Verification I was one of them. It must have been hard for Cathy to discover she was the second baby-girl-Donager to be given the name Mary Catherine at birth.

An affable cabbie dropped me at the Anatole. Frigid air replaced the humidity. Above the hotel lobby, an atrium revealed layers of ballrooms, girded with darkened steel castings and brick columns. Prison-like hotels were not my typical choice but this one provided the lap pool therapy I sought.

I extracted my swimsuit from my bag and wandered out the side entrance through a colonnade of live oaks to the fitness center. A sole survivor of the latest round of economic-downturn layoffs directed me to the pool. I dove in, breast-stroking underwater to the center line before breaking the surface to begin my hour-long routine.

At that first in-person meeting, in the neutral territory of California, Cales had ensconced himself in a poolside cabana, his eyes tracking my laps. Afterward, I had dropped into the chaise next to him.

He had squeezed my hand. "Just making sure you are real."

"Tell me again about how you knew."

"By age ten, I was fairly certain you existed." He had leaned back in his chaise, describing how he had hidden under the kitchen table, in hallway shadows, listening to his parents rip each other asunder. "So, I confronted them, but, Laney was adamant in her denial. Said she and Daddy were just arguing about a miscarriage."

I knew the rest by heart. State-sealed records kept him from pursuing a search and when the sibling registry was initiated, Diana, his wife, had pointed out I might not know I was adopted, which pushed Cales off the scent again. After a quick Jacuzzi, I headed back to my room, called Jen to check in, ordered room service and waited, expectant in spite of myself. Such expectations had never been met. No one called.

* * *

Patrick's oncologist greeted me in the outer office and led me to his cubicle, a box formed by three partitions and a window bank overlooking the endless blue sky of East Dallas. He leaned back in his chair, hands laced behind his head. "We couldn't have found a better match."

I gave up a half smile. "A medical miracle?"

He studied me. "How long have you been in Seattle?"

"Almost thirty years." His accent gave him away. "How long have you been in Dallas?"

"Fifteen. Started in research but missed the clinical side."

"Yale or Harvard?" He just had that look about him.

"Yale."

"And how many of these have you done?"

"More than a few."

"I researched Neuprogen." They would inject me with this drug every day for the next six, to mobilize the stem cells in my blood stream.

"Questions?"

I shrugged. "I'll most likely get arthritis in my old age anyway."

The Yalie laughed. "The dry wit must be hereditary. Why has Patrick not mentioned you before?"

"No one has filled you in?"

"Well, I did notice your hyphenated last name didn't include Donager."

"The senior Donagers engaged in quite a bit of extracurricular activity prior to divorcing their first spouses and marrying one another. Activities with multiple consequences, one of which was me." While the Yalie absorbed the information, two fighter jets soared above the single cloud in the blue expanse. A vapor trail streamed behind. "It feels too late to me. Odds?"

The Yalie waited for me to make eye contact. "Between ten and twenty percent."

"But Patrick's chances may be closer to the former?"

He nodded. The horizon swallowed the jets but not their out-of-the-blue wake. It's odd finding out you were the by-product, left behind, valued less than the main: my birthparent's obsession with each other. Or at least, hers. *Was I doing this to daylight their mistake?*

I touched the manila file folder that contained my completed donor form, a last-ditch effort I couldn't bring myself to refuse even though no one had actually asked me if I would do this thing. "Okay, then. What happens next?"

* * *

The days settled into a routine: injection at the medical center at 10 a.m., a cobb salad at the hotel cafe at noon, a couple of hours fielding business calls and school board emails, lap swim at three, shampoo and blow-dry by five, cocktail at six, with either an old pal or a novel in hand to stave off my own dark thoughts.

Here's the good news about granulocyte colony-stimulating factors (GCSF): you can get high on just a half a cocktail and alcohol doesn't thwart your stem cell build up. The bone aches began day four, giving credence to the other pains I was experiencing, a recycling of emotions lived out a decade prior. Emotions unresolved no matter how many laps I swam.

Day five, I met Barb and Patrick for dinner. A small blue box from Tiffany's loomed next to my place setting when I arrived. After an awkward round of hugs, I dove right in.

"Why didn't you guys let me know when this first began?"

Barb fielded the first pitch. "Patrick didn't want word getting out. Amazing how quickly clients spook if they think their representation might be afflicted."

Patrick leaned in, visibly weaker, his bulk reduced by the perpetrator. "I've still got a mortgage to pay."

"So, you were never going to tell me?"

Patrick shrunk into the booth, his discomfort from his pre-transplant regimen and my question evident.

I had done nothing but ask questions from the day I had met them. In my rush to know the entire story, I had pieced together facts that none of them wanted to hear. The biggest surprise: my birthmother, the rare 1940s businesswoman, had allowed her regional supervisor, my birthfather, to impregnate her three times before they said "I do." She miscarried the first, but not before she had filed for divorce from her first hubby. When she got pregnant again, the Donager family priest arranged for her to stay at the Home where she gave up the second, me. Then, third time being the charm and all, my birthfather finally obtained a divorce, and they got married just one month prior to Cales being born.

I asked another question. "When are you going to tell Bryn?"

Patrick hid behind his water glass.

Barb shifted in her seat. "We just wanted her to have this trip without worrying." Barb's face tightened. "The doctor was so encouraging after the first round of chemo last year, we didn't think it would be an issue. But now…" Her voice trailed off.

The waiter saved us by taking cocktail orders and handing out menus. I rubbed at the small of my back.

Patrick peered over his menu. "How are the injections going?"

"How do folks get addicted to heroin? I mean, who actually craves a daily injection?"

Patrick mustered a grin. "They call my prep a conditioning regimen. Hah! Imagine the worst, most sadistic personal trainer ever and that's my doctor."

"The Yalie?" I raised an eyebrow. "It's always the quiet ones."

Patrick took a small sip of water, but I could tell even plain water didn't sit well.

He continued. "They start with two lethal doses of chemo, followed by a batch of radiation for good measure. A buckshot approach to kill as many of the leukemia cells as possible, lest, you know, they kill me before the switcheroo."

Barb broke the ensuing silence by pushing the blue box closer to my knife. "We got you a little something."

Discomfort scaled my spine, the box and the drug side effects fueling it in equal measure. "Really not necessary."

Barb smiled her lovely smile. "It's not a small thing you are doing."

Unable to make eye contact, I pulled on the ribbon and popped off the lid. Inside rested a small velvet box and inside that was a delicate gold chain with an infinity pendant. I dangled the chain from my index finger. "It's lovely."

Patrick looked at it like it might be the first time he had seen it.

"We thought, with cells being given and all, well," Barb stumbled, forming her words. "The infinity symbol felt right."

They seemed to be waiting for it, so I slid it on my neck. But now, I was stuck, not knowing what to say and not really feeling what I thought I should be. From the time I could talk, I referred to myself as Mom's 'Dopted Darling. We used to drive past the Home, only two blocks from our Methodist church in Austin. Mom would point out the window and say, "That's where we picked you out."

A large Catholic family had lived across the street from us and when one of their teenage sons teased me about being adopted, I had stood my five-year-old-self right up to him and said, "My mother picked me out, Johnny Noack. Your mother got stuck with you!" My entire identity was rooted in being chosen, not tossed out with the bath water. But, in fact, my full-blooded birth family had rowed merrily along together, while I grew up in another. As if I would have made their boat sink. Now, I was the only one that might keep them afloat.

I raised my scotch glass. "Here's to you preferring Dewars to Jack in the very near future." Patrick smiled, but I suspected he would never buy a fifth of Scotch.

* * *

Day six rolled in. I swam my last laps before Jen collected me for the move to her house. The draw location was forty-eight hours away. Brad, Aunt Sarah's son had flown in from Savannah. Said he had to be there for all of us. Cales insisted we paltry few go out for dinner the next evening. Patrick was back in the hospital in pre-game. Diana, Cales' wife, was out of town on a gal's golf trip. Cathy would not make the drive from Bedford on a school night.

Barb and I followed the men to the restaurant in her car. We settled around a table and Cales ordered me a scotch I did not really want.

Brad sipped his vodka. "Last night, Cales listed all the times your paths could have possibly crossed at UT and after. Fascinating."

"Hot tub musings?" I asked.

Early in our relationship, Cales would often call, one in the morning his time, 11 p.m. mine, from his back-terrace Jacuzzi, a bourbon in hand, "just to hear my voice."

Brad nodded. "My favorite is the Beta match party."

"I loathed match parties." *And yet.*

Cales signaled the waiter for a second bourbon. "I'm clear we hung out next to each other that night."

"I'm unclear about that." I took a sip of my scotch, willing it to dull my back pain.

Barb weighed in, recounting in wonder how I had lived and worked in Dallas for many years, within a mile or two of most of the Donagers. I had to admit that their former proximity had a mystical timbre.

Brad twirled his ice. "What I can't get over is your Dad working at your dry cleaners."

I rankled at the word Dad. *Pierce Cales Donager, Sr. is not my dad.* After my birthfather had imploded into alcoholism, his infidelities piled up and he gambled away every cent they had and then some. Mob-backed bookies began threatening, and Cales left school to help pay off the last of the debt. My birthmother had finally called it quits, but several embarrassing incidents followed their separation, including the theft of the family silver.

Cales, barely a man himself, had picked Pierce up out of the proverbial gutter, filed for his social security, and gotten him a part-time job at the dry cleaners in my neighborhood. No doubt we stood across the two-foot counter from one another more than once. If you need further proof that there are patterns in the universe, come sit by me. Nestle into the high-backed chairs I bought from the Rattan Shop in Dallas with my first paycheck out of college. My birthmother was their bookkeeper for the second half of her life.

I rubbed my back. "Which way is the Ladies room?"

Barb motioned to her left.

Halfway down the back hallway, Cales caught up with me. "Can we just talk for a minute? Alone." He motioned toward an empty private dining room.

I smoothed my hands over the white tablecloth. "Okay. What?"

"Come on, Angel."

He had not used his pet name for me until this moment. It meant he was drunk, wrapped up in his mind-movie, me the celestial presence, him gazing upward through his film filter, waiting for me to fall. *What's the quotient of grace you need to actually fall from it?*

He put his hand over mine.

Everything about this moment was predictable except this: his touch sparked no current. I searched his eyes for the lost connection. "Look, you got what you wanted, I'm here. I just resent the assumption is all."

His surprise looked genuine. "What?"

"Did it ever occur to you, any of you, to actually ask me if I would do this?"

He blinked.

"I would not have said no. I just think someone should have asked." A tear escaped down my cheek, annoying me on a visceral level. He reached over to wipe it away, that look in his eye, but I jerked up, spooked by the lack of sensation. As if someone had unplugged us without me noticing. "I have to use the Ladies." The restroom door swung closed behind me, ushering in a short-lived relief.

Cales burst in and gathered me up in his arms before I could stop him. He kissed my cheeks, my forehead. "I'm so sorry, Angel. I'm so sorry."

I wrestled away. "What are you doing? Get out of here."

He pulled me back to his chest and whispered, "I was so afraid you would say no."

"Well, I never had that chance, did I?" My anger at the situation bumped up against something new: pity. *He is still in the movie, and I have left the theater.* I stopped fighting his hold. "Please, let me go."

"It's okay. You don't have to pretend."

"I'm not." *And, I'm not.* The electricity had short circuited at last. As if by doing this one thing, precisely because no one asked me to, I have filled the void.

Cales's arms dropped to his sides, but he didn't move.

I steadied myself against the vanity. "Go," I said, escaping into a stall.

When I returned to the table, Cales and Brad were talking Southwest Conference football. Barb looked up at me with a question in her eyes she did not voice. I picked at my food and the subject of dessert arose.

I whispered to Barb. "I need to get into the recline. My back is killing me."

She nodded, showing sympathy for more than my back. We said our goodbyes before anyone could object and drove the darkened streets in silence, wheels turning under us and in our heads.

* * *

Jen and I followed the nurse into the transplant unit. Donor beds were spaced a fair distance apart. The nurse consulted my chart. A resident appeared and began to chat with me about the implementation of a central line. I focused in horror at the woman in the bed across the room, tubes protruding from her neck.

"No one said anything about a central line. I thought this was a straightforward blood draw."

The nurse stroked my arm. "Typically, it's easier than trying to find a vein."

"I have perfectly good veins in both arms, and no one is cutting my neck open." I summoned my most commanding tone. "Call the Yalie if you have to."

The resident exchanged a look with the nurse. "Let's give it a try, shall we?"

The nurse made fast work of finding a healthy vein in both of my arms. She attached a tube on each that connected to a machine that would spin out my stem cells before my blood cycled back into me. Jen worked the pillows under my shoulders and head. An orderly wheeled in a dark metal box. Tubes looped and stretched. The machine whirred.

My blood flowed in a steady stream out of my right arm, through the clear tubing and into one side of the box. A few seconds later, blood flowed out the other side and into the tube attached to my left arm, a painless transaction that trapped me there for eight hours. I closed my eyes against the memory of last night.

Brad arrived, eager to be of service, allowing Jen to take a break. The nurse approved me having ice cream. Brad departed in search of chocolate chip. He returned and spooned it to me like I was a baby. My birthmother told me she had eaten only ice cream for a week after she had me. Her toxemia had transferred to me in the cord, causing me to run a fever for weeks after birth. *Had her decision been an attempt to spare me from further toxicity: the toxic relationship she chose over me?*

Jen returned, toting the latest Vogue. Brad said his goodbyes and left us to flip the pages of the fall-fashion preview.

I pointed at a model's forearm tattoo. "That has to be henna. Kristen McMenamy might walk in body paint for Vuitton, but she isn't going to let anyone permanently tattoo her forearm." I recounted a recent event, held in our Seattle store, that had included henna artists.

"Producing such unique events, it's a gift," Jen said.

My birthmother, according to all accounts, had thrown the best parties, the consummate hostess. It is one thing to see your physical reflection in a blood relative, but it is even more disturbing to discover your talents were also determined by genetics.

The nurse checked the counter on the machine. "Just about done."

On cue, the Yalie sidled up to my bed. "I hear you are running the show."

"My blood. My show."

"Well, curtain time. We've should have what we need. It'll take them eight or so hours to analyze the results. Anything under three million viable cells, we may need another draw."

I grimaced, feeling caged. "They'll call?"

"Around Noon tomorrow."

* * *

I piled up on Jen's living room couch, cushioning pillows against my aching back. Jen set a plate of eggs on the coffee table. "What else can I get you?"

"How can I ever thank you?"

"This huge thing you did, Mike and I are in awe." Jen tucked a napkin over me. "We would never have not been by your side."

My birthmother sent me a seven-page letter when I found her. She wrote that the priest had manipulated her, isolating her at the Home in Austin, and yet, she had gone back to my birthfather.

One part stuck with me: "I can't really explain why I gave you up. I don't know why I let myself be treated the way I did for all those years. I guess you just can't explain love."

An adoption counselor once told me that when a child is relinquished, something is very, very wrong. All my life, my adoptive parents had assured me that such an act is out of love. I believe my birthmother's decision to give me up was driven by love, some for me, but mostly for Pierce, for fear of losing him if she kept me.

The Baylor hospital number scrolled across my cell phone screen. I answered and a technician said my name.

"Yes, this is she."

"Year of birth? For ID confirmation."

"1952." A year aptly defined by "Ozzie and Harriet" and "I've Got a Secret."

"The draw was quite successful. We retrieved over five million viable stem cells."

"So, I'm free to leave?"

"Yes."

Jen walked over. "Well?"

I gave her a thumbs-up. "I'm going to see if I can change my flight to tomorrow."

* * *

Jen loaned me her car for my tenth trip to Baylor. The wing that housed Patrick burst with light from the south. Light I hoped Patrick could soak up a while longer. A nurse strung up an IV as I entered.

Patrick shot me a wry smile. "My morning cocktail."

I grasped the rail on the end of his bed. "It appears I'm a world champion donor. Doc says they can even bank some if you need back up after the first run."

His smile cracked a bit. "A backup plan is always good."

"How long are they keeping you?"

"They'll do their thing day after tomorrow. Then we shall see."

"I've got a flight out at two, but I'll check in with Barb."

Patrick held my gaze. "Listen—" His cell vibrated on the bedside table. Bryn's face flashed on the screen.

I nodded. "Go ahead."

Patrick's eyes intensified, but the thought formed on his lips slid away as he answered. "Bryn? Did you make it to Belgium?"

I lingered, watching my baby brother talk to his baby, hoping she would be able to navigate what was sure to come. I mouthed, "We can chat later." But I knew we wouldn't.

Patrick held up a hand in protest, but I was already halfway out the door. I tossed him a fleeting smile, clipped down the corridor, took the stairs to ground level, and pushed into the heat of the day.

* * *

A note arrived from Cales's wife, Diana, thanking me for what I had done for Patrick. Cales had often fantasized that if I had been there, if we had been raised together, the two of us could have somehow altered history, not let my birthmother sign away her house to the bookies threatening physical harm. I had responded that then, there would have been no lost child to drive the marital discord, no grief or shame to feed his parents destructive behavior. I did not say that the initial lie, the affair, had weakened their chances from the start. It sealed their fate long before my birth.

Maybe, somehow, in that moment, signing those adoption papers, my birthmother thought she should save me from what was to come, if not herself. *Maybe.* In her letter, my birthmother said she had no answers, but that is mine. *I got saved.*

I nestled into one of the rattan chairs on the sunporch and propped my feet on the other, fingering Diana's note. A jet trail scraped the Seattle sky, a wisp of fading white against an otherwise clear horizon. Diana was wrong. I did not do it for Patrick. I did it for me.

Theory of Evolution: A Critique
By Sarah Grace Goolden

—After all,
not all that glitters is a metaphor.

Sometimes summer breezes by like a stranger
& it is simply an axis doing what an axis must.

What is there to say except
your planet may be laborer to unethical continuity

but he died
& it was an extinction that will scar science:

flora & fauna curling into a fist, ecosystems collapsing
from unbalance.   Did you hear the yellow core

burble nervously, unsure how to keep warm
without his honeyed laugh?

I am a couple billion years too young
to lie to myself & call it strength.

Selected Poems by Sasha Leshner

How Eve Would Speak of Paradise

I used to count your heartbeat in the evenings
to know if you were going down too low.
We went like birdsong into landmines   until I came up alone.

　　　　But I don't want to write our ballad—
I want to rename all our animals: addiction,
violence, poverty. Forgiveness. I call them

and they are too wild to even answer.
Like we forgot to paint the mouths onto a
wooden carousel of horses.

The Visible World

some people are born weapon-hearted

they see with one eye sparrowing
for permission

to take their hands out of the blue
pool of the every living
thing we're all born into

to be drawn closer to the darker
heart of any accident
or the evil of true things

like crows
or like punishment
like words that tear you out

of your own mouth
for what they fly from

because if you promise
you're going to take it
from me and it won't matter

whether I like it or not
(and I like it)

I'm capable of drawing
a cold line between
my actions and the delusion

that I can be anything
I want
if I just let myself have at it

It's a wickedness
that starts in childhood

when the snowing darkness
of your bedroom
stops being anything as scary

as the house it presses into
and the little people in it
what they do and do not

mean and the apology
as ritual
so I had to be so sorry

so I had to be just as edged
with silver

where the closing gap between
my body and the being better
than I have to

be only makes it easier
when anyways and all the time
I find I am not angelic

pretending I don't
keep secrets for myself
to feast on later

with this hunger
that never comes for me
but stings

the world I wanted
with the same ruin
I would wake in

where without such arms
to hold me

I am angled like
an arrow
and just as hard to see

Selected Poems by Zachary Kluckman

Discovery of an Unmarked Grave Near the Beach

If not for the sound of ocean, let's turn this skull
on its side and wash our feet in the runaway water.

At least this is what I assume drowning to sound
like, the swell of tides so sublime you simply cannot

tell the moon's pull from the pulse of your own heart
beat. They say there is a simple music in surrender,

in letting go of everything landlocked, like footsteps.
The proof we have walked some vague line in the sand.

In school they taught us that those who do not learn
from history are doomed to repeat it, so what

have we learned, Grandfather? Mother? What
have we taken away from all of this, from the war

and the hatred? Do we not still sling arrows across fences,
attempt to kill our neighbors because their gardens will

make beautiful graveyards? Water the flowers then.
Fill a vessel with water, that life giving holy fluid, use

this skull ironically, to measure the life we pour
into the ground. Wonder at the magic of your own hands

but consider, life exists in spite of us, not because of
us, our dirty hands, our bloody hands, our hands like shovels

digging grave after grave, the notes of a song, falling.

If you hold your ear up to another man's chest

you can hear.

Scene from a Trailer in Northern New Mexico

They found her because the dog was hungry.

His ribs began to show,
laying day after day on the porch.

Eventually their concern for the dog
led her neighbor to call someone. Bring the police.
Your mother, two months gone, lay next to
her pills. Not suicide, they assure you.

Proof she was finally getting some help.

Two months alone on her floor. Heart
destroyed by smoke. Maybe the cigarettes.
Maybe the lack of phone calls. Maybe she needed
a hug. Bent over her hurt, you picture her

stretching for the phone, wonder whose name
she called out. Yours or your sister's.

If either. Or if she was so alone with her fear
even the names would not come.

Imagine your grief is a button, a friend says,
inside of a box and someone has dropped a ball
Inside. At first it ricochets off the walls so fast
the button is constantly pressed. Over time

the ball will bounce with less force, press
your button less often until it stops.

You say, imagine grief was my mother's heart.
That's what the pills were for.

You say, they found her
because the dog was hungry.

You say,
no one knew   for two months.

You say—

Let the Dying Dog Dig
By Taylor Leigh Harper

For about a week, we blamed the heatwave: our dog Barnaby's panting, his unusual lethargy, a sudden disinterest in food, in play, in us. But even after we ran the air conditioner throughout the day, into the night, and added extra ice to his water, Barnaby remained deflated, and relief still hadn't come.

On the way to the vet, my wife said she'd noticed him coughing more since May.

"Since May?" I asked. I added this to the list of symptoms bullet pointed on my phone. "Why are you just telling me now?"

"You mean you didn't notice?" Andi turned a sharp right on a red without signaling.

The coughing, the increasing panting, his decreasing appetite. The vet—fresh, excited, eager to diagnose, pleased to provide answers—listed off Barnaby's symptoms like a practiced litany. "Heart disease is common in Boxers," the vet concluded, arriving at this with clinical certainty.

He could have said, "There's nothing you can do to reverse this."

He might have told us it wasn't our fault.

He should have reminded us that this, like all things, is natural, expected, inevitable. Everything lives briefly, seeking joy and yearning for connection, and then returns to the dirt.

Instead, the vet told us it wasn't time just yet, and gave us a list of medications to make Barnaby as comfortable as possible until that time did come. The receptionist handed us the long bill and a large brown paper bag, weighty with our dog's new pills and syringes and syrupy yellow liquids.

"See you next time," the nurse said, and she smiled so sweetly I thought about giving her Barnaby, giving her our house, giving her Andi, giving her all of this, because she might bear it better.

On the drive home, Barnaby snorted, dozing off. I gripped his graying fur. "Good boy," I said.

Andi glanced at me, saying nothing, as she glided through the yellow light.

Before the end of the season, we will have spent most of our year's savings on a few weeks' worth of borrowed time.

Barnaby's appointments were constant, at least twice a week. We called every heart specialist on the west side of Los Angeles with more than three and a half stars on Yelp, but none could see us sooner than twelve weeks out.

"Twelve weeks?" I heard my mother's voice echoed in my shrill repetition. "I won't have a dog for you to see in twelve weeks."

Someone recommended a new clinic in the valley. Andi carpooled with me during the first week of appointments. She sat in the backseat so she could be closer to Barnaby, who slept in the trunk of our SUV. With one hand, she responded to work emails, and rested her other hand over the seat against Barnaby's crate. I wished she had reached out to grab my hand, to rub my arm, to squeeze my leg. Had she put her hands anywhere on me—covered my face, traced my neck, tickled my side—I would have welcomed swerving the car.

"I can't do this," she started off saying.

"It's not my fault the traffic is stop and go," I said, rolling down the windows. "Put your head between your legs if you're feeling nauseated."

"We can't do this. All these appointments. We can't drive three, four, five hours a day twice a week."

But there were no other vets available. We had to keep an eye on Barnaby, had to learn to spell and pronounce and understand *dilated cardiomyopathy*. We had to do this.

I wiped sweat from my face and turned the AC higher. "You don't have to come."

Andi turned pale in the waiting room. "I don't do well with sickness," she said, as if any of us do. But I knew what she meant— her mother had died when she was in preschool, a sudden brain hemorrhage, and her father a few years later from an aggressive lung cancer. Andi clung to life more out of fear of dying than a love of living. Everything she did was hurried, racing away from some shadowed boogeyman.

When Doctor Shepherd finally called us back, my wife leaned against the office's cold white wall. Andi's hand went limp in mine while this vet repeated back to us what the first one had told us.

Finally, she said, "This is not uncommon in his breed. It's a strict regimen of medications. Do you have pet insurance?" Barnaby, drooling as he paced the room, began sniffing Doctor Shepherd's shoes. He pawed at her big toe.

Looking at the ceiling, Andi asked, "Do people ever put them down at this stage?"

I yanked my hand from hers.

Andi asked again, "Is that more humane?"

Doctor Shepherd kneeled down to meet Barnaby on the floor. He jumped up on her thighs, his tail wagging quicker than we'd seen in weeks. "All things considered, he is otherwise healthy. We're not quite in that gray area yet," she said. Softly, she added, "But the choice is yours."

"We're not putting him down," I said. I willed Andi to look at me. To stop staring at the ceiling, unmoving and unchanging and completely ordinary.

"It's also important to remember this is neither preventive nor curable," Doctor Shepherd said, cupping Barnaby's chin in her hands. "Your dog is dying. But you can make him comfortable. There's still time left for good days."

After that, Andi stopped coming. We came to a new unspoken agreement to split responsibilities. She handled Barnaby's old routine—his morning and evening walks, regular mealtimes without adjusting portions, his weekly dry shampoo bath—and I memorized the dosages of each medication, Doctor Shepherd's emergency number, the amount of gray fur between his shoulder blades, how clear his eyes looked at the end of each day.

Even through the night, the heat persisted. Our living room trapped the stagnant air, a hotbox of sweat and a permanent feeling of fever.

The first time I fell asleep on the couch with Barnaby sleeping on the floor, Andi spread a spare bed sheet over me, covering me ghostlike. When I woke up, disoriented with a kink in my neck, the house was dark, and Barnaby was gone.

The door leading to the backyard was open, but the screen door was still closed, a desperate attempt at beckoning a breeze. In the dark, the concrete patio looked as if it were a dock stretching out into the blue grass. The sprinklers clicked on, water bursting with a hiss.

Barnaby had not escaped. He had followed Andi upstairs into our bedroom and climbed into bed next to her.

Every night after, he slept beside Andi. On the couch, I found pillows from the guest room stacked on top of an extra blanket, folded carefully.

"I thought you might be more comfortable here," Andi said. "While Barnaby sleeps with me. Until this heat breaks."

"The bed is big enough for us all," I said.

"If that's what you want," she said, already climbing back toward our room, which had suddenly become hers alone.

In the evenings, we ate our dinner in front of the TV, old *Real Housewives* episodes auto playing through seasons while we each stared at our phones. I sat on the floor next to Barnaby, who looked into my lap for crumbed offerings. Andi sat on the couch with her knees pulled tight to her chest, answering work emails after hours, circling back to budget approval requests on hold and editing event project proposals.

I could picture her elsewhere, projecting herself away from all of this, escaping into the design of a client's perfect destination proposal, barnyard weddings in the Midwest, coastal vow renewals plush with sea breeze, white sand, and long, gauzy bridal trains. In these fairytales, there was no death, no endings, no need for a cure inside of a homebrewed potion. Love was only the salve, never the slow poison.

She'd planned our wedding. Small, in the garden behind her childhood church. My parents, older sister and brother, and grandparents cooled themselves with paper fans, and no one mentioned when Andi's only living relative—John, a conservative younger brother still in theology school—left before we finished our vows, sealing our union with a careful kiss. Everyone agreed Barnaby the ring bearer had been the day's highlight.

I'd opened my work email only to promptly close it again. School was out on break for another five weeks, but I hadn't started any of my lesson planning or revisions. The thought of going back to a classroom for eight hours a day was nauseating. I pictured myself asking a room full of kindergarteners how their summers had been—*Good, Ms. T—It was awesome, Ms. T—Ms. T, I went to Disneyland!—I swam all summer long—We chased fireflies in the dark—My parents, who love each other almost as much as they respect one another, stayed happily married, and bought me a new Barbie dreamhouse for being so darling—The summer was perfect, Ms. T.*

If any of them looked at me long enough, registering that I too was a person outside of the classroom, to ask how my summer was, I would tell them it was great.

I looked at my dying dog sitting at the front door, staring at nothing, off elsewhere, somewhere greener and cooler and more open. I looked at my wife sitting in a hard silence, thumb in mouth as she chewed on a hangnail. The wind outside was stiffening over an underbelly of sidewalk-sizzled anger, some distant helplessness approaching with a violent, obvious warning. The summer our lives fell apart was great, I would say with a smile and turn back toward the whiteboard to write the alphabet out in big block letters.

Near the end, Barnaby seemed more like himself, as if he caught a second wind of life. He'd clunk himself down the stairs, rested after a night beside Andi, and paw me awake for an early breakfast. I hid his first dose of heart medication in a piece of cheese. Barnaby, blissful and oblivious, only looked to me asking for more.

Sometimes Barnaby would then go bounding through the house, racing up and down the hallway, chasing an invisible target. He'd get himself worked up, stop to pant, before running again toward the stairs, up which he'd run right back to Andi's room.

I was afraid to follow him. I had gone up only once, trying to keep him from waking Andi on an early weekend morning, and felt I had entered someone else's home. I stood at the top of the stairs feeling awkward and embarrassed, as if I didn't know where the bathroom was, or if I had to ask someone for a cup of water. When I looked into the main room at the end of the hall, Barnaby stood at the foot of the bed, pawing to be picked up. Andi slept on, her dark hair piled on top of her head, her skin pressed deep into the sheets.

Next to Barnaby on the floor, in plain sight, were two suitcases. Stacks of clean underwear, socks, and pajamas were folded on top of them, ready to be packed.

I said Andi's name, flat and plain, and she sat up in bed as if she hadn't just been asleep. Briefly, sleep still heavy in her, she gave me something almost like a look of love.

Then Barnaby, seeing her awake, began barking, jumping, wagging his whole body. Andi clapped her hands, and Barnaby jumped into her arms.

"Good morning," she said, more to him than to me.

I stared at what she hadn't told me, but so promptly unraveled before me: she was leaving us.

"I think I might go stay with John next weekend," Andi said. "Just get out of the house for a bit."

An image of her brother flashed before me—his soft jaw and small, cruel eyes. How that gaze remained cold, no matter at whom he looked: his wife, his children, his only sister. But to reject Andi outright would be to lose what remaining family he had, sin or not.

So, he settled on refusing to grant me even a glance. Not when Andi first introduced me to him at her awkward, intimate graduation dinner, the patio's string lights sharp and ready for an interrogation. Not over the years at birthdays, holidays, or the children's baptisms. Without acknowledging me, I might as well have not been there, and his sister may yet reach out to his ever-extended hand and take the simple, straight life he wanted for her. A bubble-wrapped future where nothing and no one could ever hurt them, hurt the other.

John and Andi were so unlike, but in this way, they were identical in their will to shape more comfortable, safer realities, parables or psalms. This was why Andi, all the same, would return to him, even when she didn't like him—because she loved that he was as steadfast as he was unkind.

"But Barnaby," I tried. "He seems to be doing better, don't you think?"

She stared at us, her dying dog and wife, and smiled again. Her voice was gentle and quiet. "We can't prolong this forever."

"Really," I said, calling her bluff before I was sure that was all it was. "This is how it goes? You can't just leave."

"That's the problem," Andi said. She buried her face in Barnaby's side, and he licked her hand. "Barnaby's been sick for a while now. But I've been unhappier even longer."

"About what, Andi? I know these last few weeks have been hard, but isn't our life what you wanted?"

I meant the tomatoes we grew out back in the spring. The week we spent in Portland around the holidays, the rain so cold our toes turned white. Our bedroom, the cream duvet still soft even after

Barnaby rubbed himself all over it, and the wall of photographs that watched me now. See our wedding day, see us at the top of Fern Canyon, see my mother with her arms around Andi one autumn evening, a carved pumpkin grinning so wide and unaware.

"I feel like you don't see us for what we are. He's dying," she said. "And I'm unhappy."

I wanted to tell her I saw them as they were—dying and unhappy, but also still alive, still full of wonder, still mine, ours, together.

But I sensed in myself a rising tantrum, a gurgling cry and hot, snotty fit. If I threw myself down, offered my apologies, surrendered my stubbornness to cling to what was already going, could I make them stay a little longer?

Barnaby looked back at me standing in silence. He scratched his ear, tilted his head, and sighed, all but saying you cannot make someone hold on who has already let go, who is half here and half elsewhere, entirely gone and still going further.

That was not the first time Andi left. Late one spring, when I was in the last year of my graduate program and working on weekends at a nearby Sunday school, I came home to a letter in an unlicked envelope.

In my dreams, Andi wrote, her perfect handwriting sharp and slanted, *we are never older than when we first met.*

When we first met, her hair was buzzed short, dyed blue-black. She was backstage, situating props for our college's performance of *Macbeth.* I came around looking for my roommate, Nina, who I wasn't in love with, but wanted to be in love with me—to see me not just when she asked if she could borrow my going-out tops or eat my cold dining hall leftovers.

"Lady Macduff?" The prop designer barely glanced at me before resuming tying a garland of paper leaves. "She was here. Somewhere. She's not on until the fourth act."

"I just wanted to give her these," I said, holding the day's old bouquet of tulips toward her. Then she looked at me—her face was round, chin soft, and her eyes met mine briefly before shifting back to the flowers.

"Can I see those?"

In an instant, they were hers, and she plucked the long limp leaves off one by one. "That's it," she said, not to me, lacing them into the garlands. "Something real. Something with a bit of life."

I asked her name.

"Andi," she said. "I'll tell Lady Macduff you brought these, but I needed them more. If she doesn't understand, I owe you five bucks."

In her dreams, we were still on the cusp of determined youth. *We never get older,* she wrote repeatedly, as if by will she could make it true. *We never get sick. You're safe. You're safe. You're safe.*

Later, when I found her—a weekend's worth of clothes and toiletries neatly laid out in her brother's family's guest room—she shrugged, as if coming out of a daze. "Sometimes I get worried you'll leave me first. You'll go to work, and won't come back, and it'll just be me in the house by myself forever. So, I just thought I'd see what it felt like. Where I might have to go to not be alone again." The bareness of the room John made up for her was dizzying.

I couldn't bring myself to talk about the letter. What she had written and confessed went unmentioned between us, even when we saw a therapist together a week later. Andi remained calm while she recounted growing up without her parents, and even kept a straight face throughout her re-explanation of why she'd left our apartment without so much as a phone call. But when our therapist asked Andi how it made her feel that I'd come looking for her, she looked up at the ceiling and blinked quickly.

"It made me feel like the thing I feared most losing loved me, too." Andi pressed her palms against her flush cheeks. "But that made me feel worse in some ways. Like it was all too much to bear."

"What was?" I asked at the same time as the therapist.

"All of this," she said only to the therapist. "This love. But mostly this fear."

After Andi went back to her brother's house, the days lost distinction, marked only by Barnaby's continued strict combination of medications. My wife's absence made the stuffy house unbearable—she was nowhere Barnaby looked, crawling low to the ground, sniffing under closet doors and behind furniture, like Andi was playing some long game of hide-and-seek.

Doctor Shepherd kept her voice level when she told me we were closer to the end than we had been at the last appointment. "There's still fluid in Barnaby's lungs," she said, and I wished she would cup my face as she held his then. "We can drain it again, but it will keep filling up—maybe not tomorrow, maybe not the day after. But we're talking a few weeks at most, if that."

We hadn't yet talked about if we wanted Barnaby cremated. I wanted to ask Andi, if we did, who would keep his ashes—*you or me?*—but the "or" reverberated in me, electric and lonely.

Barnaby watched me, cocking his head. Quietly, I asked the vet if we could please try. "Just once more," I said, and I couldn't look at her or Barnaby as I stepped over a threshold of selfishness I knew from which I could not turn back.

That last time Barnaby had the fluid drained from his lungs, we returned home both defeated. Our eyes glazed over whatever afternoon news ran across the television. Andi texted me excerpts of her brother's weekend observations, her sister-in-law's passive aggression, and her nieces' peculiar food fixations.

john thinks sleeping in on a sat is sloth

surprise! Norah's single cousin is still single…

maria and elaine only want to eat jelly toast with raisins

I called Andi. She answered on the fourth ring. "Would you?"

"Would I what?" Her voice was quiet. I heard a door close behind her. I imagined her in that dark, air-conditioned guest room, the walls bare save for a single wooden cross above the headboard.

I wanted to ask her if she would take her sister-in-law's bait—if she would show any interest in this single cousin Norah brought up every time she saw Andi. If it wouldn't be so frightening to love this cousin. If maybe this cousin could save Barnaby. If this cousin would've not only noticed the first signs of sickness back in May, but if he would have done something about it sooner. "Would you eat jelly toast with raisins?"

"Believe me," Andi said. "I already have. It's not as bad as you might think."

We waited for the other to think of something to say. When neither of us could, we sat a bit longer in the quiet. Andi sniffled.

Barnaby, spent and sleepy, rested his jowls on my chest, and sighed. My phone buzzed, the battery dying.

"How's he doing?" Andi finally asked.

"Same as yesterday." I strained the lie, sifting for a pebble of truth that I could use to delude myself.

"Sometimes at night, I'll wake up, and the first thing I check is that he's still breathing. Even when it's dark, I know where he is, right next to me, his head on your pillow, and I put my hands on his chest. And even when I feel him rise and fall, I'm still not sure it's real, so I'll shake him, just slightly, to make sure he's still there. And he always is."

I didn't remind Andi she had woken me more than once doing something similar to me—a light shake of the shoulder, so careful and trepid I initially passed it off as her brushing me in her sleep. But I learned to roll toward her when this happened, place my arm around her and bury my face in her chest, breath warm from my nose against her clammy skin.

"Do you ever feel like you're mourning him before he's gone?" she asked.

"All the time," I said. "When we first took him to the vet, when that doctor said there wasn't anything we could do to cure him, I tried to picture our lives without him. My clothes without the smell of his saliva. Our bags and cords no longer chewed. What it would sound like coming home, to call out his name and not have him dancing at the door."

"That emptiness," Andi said. "How does it not frighten you?"

I thought of the bedroom upstairs that I still hadn't slept in for weeks. That long, dark hallway, lined with closed doors and stale shadows. "I am so scared," I said. "And I am so sad. I bear it for him, though. I'm petting him now. We're lying on the floor in the kitchen. He smells so rank—he needs a bath. I never thought I'd miss bath time, the wet fur and soapy mess. His eyes are closed, and he looks so happy. Maybe he isn't. I hope he's not in pain. But I do it for him."

"I see," was all Andi said. Then we listened to each other cry before Barnaby eventually got up and pawed at the back door to go out into the world, to swim in the sun just a bit longer.

I let Barnaby dig in the backyard while he still could. We had never allowed him to dig before, carefully watching him whenever he did play outside. Our boy was always mild-mannered and obedient, though, so it didn't take long for him to stop trying.

The Saturday afternoon sun, cruel and bright at the top of the sky, made us both lazy. I didn't want to take him for a walk around the neighborhood, and Barnaby didn't want to go further than the end of the driveway.

His excavation left nothing rooted. Up came grass, weedy dandelions, soil dried out from the long, never-ending summer. While he chased a butterfly low to the ground, I called Andi again.

"Are you coming back?" I asked, trying to be casual, as if she had just been gone longer at the store than usual. I thought I felt a breeze. I thought maybe I heard a car door close, the quiet rumble of an engine turning on.

"I didn't think I would miss him this much," she said.

Barnaby destroyed the backyard, tearing up earth from earth, rooty dirt flung across the grass. There were shallow holes across the lawn, little graves or openings for something new to be planted. Even he seemed shocked to take in what had been done, pausing by my side. The phone felt hot against my cheek. "He's still here," I said.

Again, Barnaby went running, the world open and wide for him to embrace. In the photo I sent to Andi, he was a blur, a dark rush of fur lighted by an orange glow. My wife laughed, asking what happened to the yard, what had he done, who would clean up the mess?

I met Barnaby in the grass. The dirt was soft against my skin as I laid down among it. Barnaby followed, towering over me as he sniffed my face.

"Maybe," Andi said. "Maybe if we stay just like this."

Her thought remained unfinished. But I waited. So long, that the sun began to dip behind the brick wall. Barnaby lay down next to me for a while, before bringing me offerings: a small rock, a wet wad of grass, an old, deflated ball that had been lost behind a bush.

"Come home, Andi," I finally said, the sky darkening still, Barnaby dozing off before dinnertime. I felt myself covered in mosquito bites, itchy welts pocketing all-exposed skin.

I was almost certain I heard the turn signal of her car clicking. A distant car horn honking. Andi humming some lovely song, her arrival approaching.

Like the sky above, my phone had gone dark, dead and silent.

Still, I repeated myself. "Come home, come home, come home."

Back to me and these dandelions, hemlock, astroturf, wet mortar, landscaping rocks and pebbles. Back to this terrible pause and rush of our lives, directionless and uncertain, too hot and uncomfortable to stay still long enough to appreciate the present tense. Back to our bedroom, our living room, our shared lives, our chests rising, falling, rising in the long dark of night.

Back to Barnaby, his eyes wet with delight as he panted beside me. He showed no signs of fear, no look of knowing that he was dying, that things were changing, if not completely ending.

Then, he was still here—whether I mourned him now or later, he looked up at the sweep of sky and stretched.

I rolled over in the grass. Porch lights turned on, a dull yellow glaze over the wall. I placed my dead phone in one of Barnaby's dig spots. Slowly, I scooped dirt over the phone until a layer covered the screen.

Barnaby rolled over, too, his belly exposed.

"Come here, boy," I called, not waiting to see if he would get up before I began unburying another shallow pit in the earth. A shared sense of urgency licked in the air. Between us and the other side, there was only time and gravel-thick layers of this summer dirt. We would dig all night long if we needed to, waiting for Andi or the end, whoever returned first.

The Broken Backs of Mosaics
By Haley Wilson

Maybe they're right about all of it,
Maybe there's no point to the melee of it—
the madness of it.

Maybe the bruises are supposed to bury us.
Maybe sunders aren't meant to be mended,
but if sutures make survivors
There might be time.

If Humility breeds strength,
rather than the frailty I was promised,
and if beatings turned me sunken,
not Hollowed,
There might be time.

If there isn't though,
and if these shambles are wreckage
and not Mosaic shards,

then i will never catch the Light,
held together by depth and brevity
all at once.
i'll remain shattered at Their feet.

One of Two
By Erika B. Girard

I am from the Tide
laundry detergent box, once a liquid
      paired with a twin in a Bounce
fabric softener blanket, both swaddled:
two halves of the same whole.

        Together we are one.

One like the rolled-up posters sitting in
      the closet, no longer needing elastics to
hold them   they are perpetual scrolls,
      relics of Scholastic book fairs long past,
blank checks and colorful erasers

lost among oak trees, blanket of fallen leaves around
this home fallen, falling, falling slowly—
      easy and hard to catch, simultaneously
undefinable and steady, these columns
smaller than we imagined them to be. Our trunks

of hoarded memories remain downstairs
      in the cellar   where I grew up riding
a tricycle, only a tricycle because my father
      never taught me how to ride

a singular object with *two* wheels.

Thursday at the Heard Museum
By Christian Paulisich

> *"What I see is my home. I don't own it but it's home—the*
> *river, the trees, the birds that fly, they're all mine."*
> *~Estefanita Martinez, San Juan Tewa*

I

M and I drive through Phoenix, early June, 102
    degrees, no wind, saguaros
flanking the roadside like prickly lampposts.

Last night, a coyote, wasted-to-bone,
   scrambled through yet another
suburban development: houses hardly
     Southwestern, without Spanish red
roofs, and so much more room than any Native
would be granted on this sandy stretch

of land.

II

The first hallway is lined with walking sticks: limbs

    chopped and smoothed over, adorned

with vibrant beads, coyote fur, leather left to sit in the sun.

To the right are replicas of Native men, fun-sized,

    horseback, blades drawn,

and it's nice to imagine the land chockfull

of buffalo, wildflowers, ferns, feathered friends and

can you hear it?

   Wind slicing the meadow, rumble of river rocks below the
gorge.

Before the shock of bullets,

        my ancestors stationed within margins

not much larger than this glass case.

III

Barrage of turquoise and lapis lazuli set into jewelry worn by chiefs.

To the left, Hopi wedding garb and photos of Native women worn
soft with grief, after husbands and brothers were hanged

under the sun like Navajo rugs displayed
in the next exhibit: my people's products sold
for thousands to self-proclaimed "wokes,"
"well-cultured collectors of indigenous works."

They bring the blankets home
to their splotch of suburbia.

IV

We make it to the end, an exhibit titled *HOME*.
        I ask M what a home even is, your home,
my home, is it more than the bricks, the foundation,
        the people trapped within these walls?
We read the wallpaper; history held
        captive in the mind's eye.

Treaties and contracts broken
        like silence

by the frypan's popping oil, the system of reservations,
        assimilation, the ritual cleansing
of the *Indian character*—children shipped to boarding schools,
        and here, on display, a barber's seat
and human hair sheared
        and scattered on the cold tile.
There's a man staring at me as I wait
        for the black locks to breathe
back at me.

Did they do this to my *bisabuelo*, his family?
        Did he escape by luck? Wit?
A Spanish surname?
        Interracial marriage? Still,
the odd man stands in front of me, staring, held captive
        by his own reflection.

V

My great-grandfather moved from Taos
to a suburb by the San Francisco Bay.
Not as far as I from his native land,
nevertheless, his bags packed with ambition,
he made a home the way all Natives do: out of nothing
but his spirit, his heritage, his body.
So why can't I?

Selected Poems by Allison Collins

At the Chorus Concert

I was late getting there,
had to comb the rows of heads and duck, apologetically,
into the single seat saved on the end
as a box-chested woman doled out thank-yous and plaudits.
My husband shifted a coat,
lifting some lid,
never knowing how close
he'd positioned me
to ruin.

I wonder, dimly, if ever I could sit
in a darkened auditorium
and not know your shape,
even from behind.
But I can't answer my own musings,
too busy am I wanting to bite your neck.

I am breathless from the dash
to this place,
but also seeing you;
it still carries the thrill
I know it shouldn't,
like lovemaking in a church.

Ours was a soap-bubble moment
(though nothing so clean as that)
and dissolution the condition of
getting to be.

The children—our children!—are taking turns now,
coming forward, reading from

small slips of paper to introduce the song
and it squawks, the mic, but it's not that
that makes me flinch.

I finger the paper program in my lap
but really I'm working the tatty pleats
of this map,
the one kept in my head, penciled
with a route, a path, a trailhead
leading through the impossible ruts
of time and circumstance
back to you.

You don't know it, but this is a topography
I travel often, too often.
It is, really,
all nihilistic ravines and tortured cliff faces
tamed, made talismanic
by memory and longing.
No one would ever call me intrepid, outdoorsy
but here I am, a mountaineer.

Then, I was a head-thrown laugh,
a body piscine and unhemmed-in
by carpool lanes, thickets of high-pile carpeting,
this landscape of laundry.

Then, I was elastic, made for dancing,
a thing reeled and reeling.
You pulled me close enough
I could smell the onion on your breath
and I didn't even mind,
that or the country music,
so different from the song playing now.

The Diving Horse

It was the kind of place with paint peeling
from the faces of leering cartoon statues,
ancient creaking kiddie rides,
AstroTurf walkways and
ten-dollar cotton candy—
someone's last-ditch effort to
keep another generation's
balloon dreams afloat.

I don't know why we went.
(*Memories! Fun!*)
The air smelled of sunscreen,
sugar, stale bodies.

There was a diving horse,
all doorknob knees
and square yellow teeth.

I think, sometimes, about what came before—
what race it failed to run,
what cut-rate circus ring it circled,
what hard-up farmer weighed
forfeiting it to this farce
against handgun-made meat—
consumption, all.

Queuing with the others,
a mass of bumping stroller wheels
and sticky tugging hands,
I felt guilt.
Felt party to something
unstoppable,
condemning it, as we were, to the performance;
a show not so different, really,

from other dramas.

Still, I watched.
Heard the handler click and cajole
the long way up ladder rungs
until hooves met ledge,
the horse pawing the soft
rotten wood of the platform,
slicked in the moldering rime of
fear and repetition.

I think of that horse now
as I spread my own arms wide and,
wild-eyed, chin tipped,
toe the edge of … *what?*
My life? The carefully amassed trappings
that have become, simply, traps?
Oh, to be unbridled.

But when it leapt, when it hurtled
that impossible body,
muscled and furred and,
for that breath,
sun-burnished,
I gasped right along with the rest,
watched its tail made comet
and clapped.

The Moon is Rhyming with Every Star
By David Park

Tonight the moon is out in all its glory
rhyming
with every star
and the wind is banging on things
twisting sounds and silences inside out and backwards
the sky groaning   stretching from horizon to horizon
the animals are worked up
keeping the beat
getting the message loud and clear
and calling back to the heavens
in a sonic salad of languages
humble beasts coming out of hiding
and the few humans
brave and curious enough to be standing out here
in this circle of space
minus their telescopes and their dictionaries
are trying to take it all in
to catch the drift
are straining to hear everything
straining to catch what's between the lines
and between what beams of light are shining through the dark
even trying to join in
and touch the sky
like they did when they were young with one eye closed
and no formal knowledge of astronomy
or even words
like this is one big multilingual slam poetry extravaganza
in the fertile dark
verses being born
and the moon and stars and wind go on and on 'til dawn

all rubbing against each other
sparking emotion
waiting for us to look up and snap our fingers.

Selected Poems by Darlene Montonaro

Non, Je Ne Regrette Rien
for *Edith Piaf*

At the salon in the chair beside me
the subject has turned to tats. The smell
of coconut shampoo and a cloud of hairspray
separate us, as I pretend to read
my magazine—bony long-faced models
with blue spikes and disheveled hair.
The patrons gather, bare their wrists,
drop smocks to expose a pale shoulder.

The blow dryer drones. From beneath
the sheath of her cape, Trudy wrestles
a beefy arm, her name flamboyantly
embroidered from knuckle to elbow.
She separates from the black plastic,
opens her shirt, draws her hand
across the braille of her drooping breasts.
Her motto—*I REGRET NOTHING.*

I think of Trudy's lovers, fingers tracing
each ascender and descender, she already forgiving
their clumsiness, the droop and drag
of skin, the yeasty smell of beer.
In this house of mirrors, I cannot escape
my pale skin, unmarked but for scars unremarkable,
the only wildness my graying, non-compliant hair.

Later, I'll stand at the mirror and search
to be sure it's not there, stenciled faintly

at the small of my back—my own insignia,
I was afraid of everything. I'll remember Piaf,
stark and beautiful on an empty stage, her face
expressionless, her voice like a needle
stinging my unpierced ears.

In Strawberry Season

Always, in the strawberry days of June
we packed our gear and headed west
stopping the car to gather wild fruit
in bowls we pulled from our backpacks.
Beside icy streams released by spring
we spread blankets, lazed with other travelers,
passed demi-johns of homemade wine
under stars brighter than we had ever seen.

You fed carrots to wild horses, painted
fields of flowers. I collected river stones,
wrote poems, sang off-key to Joplin
gone sour with love. This was strawberry season,
hands and pens and brushes sickly sweet
with the hopefulness of summer.

There are times I forget, times I realize
I am stuck in the wrong room of memory
wandering a place like those abandoned mining towns
we drove out of our way to find. The sadness
of weathered buildings, everything frozen in mid-gesture—
a table of grinning outlaws, a hand
permanently raised to drink. Inhabitants
only shades, like the shadow people
who gathered around you at the end.

In the abandoned streets I hear the faint strain
of Rod Stewart's tin-pan piano, feel the hard hit
of whiskey that takes your breath away,
taste again the grit of sour and sweet.

Selected Poems by Rachel Azona Warshaw

ode to my mother's suncrest peaches from the summer of 2019

My mother cans peaches every year,
hauls a crate to the farmers' market, asks the orchards
to corral the sun into a weight that can be bought,
like the trees' boughs heavy with saccharine potential
can be counted, atoned for, redistributed,
and sung of. Here is a sweetness in perpetuity:

my mother called me on the phone today,
said: "We've been eating last year's peaches.
Remember when I could barely stand for pain?
Remember the twinge of broken ribs, a pierced spleen?
Remember when I was so afraid I couldn't can?
Last year's peaches taste like recovery,
like a straight back held strong again,
like a promise that the years heal as much as they hurt."

I relish the pop of the sealed lid being opened,
the slow drip of the canning syrup swirling out
of the mason jars we took from Grandma Tanse's basement.
How marvelous, to taste the sun
even in this winter
of our discontent,
this chilling time.

bury your gaze

I keep a store of shadows,
collection against solitude,
a purse of promises,
uttered at night.

My heart has been throwing itself against the windows,
a clear barrier against affection,
a look, but don't touch,
kind of protection.

Bury your gaze,
look not upon this scaffolding
where I hang my flesh and hope someone sees
behind the curtain, the hidden man,
the shadows, the beating, tale-telling,
coward heart.

I beckon, beacon,
bright angel for days,
and pray to catch your gaze.

Contours
By Marie-Andree Auclair

I like to think my cup waits for me, plain and smooth,
fat and white, that it waits, empty, open.

On cold mornings, I condition it, fill its hollow
with hot water, so coffee retains its heat.

I shape my hands to the cup's girth—
its form, a practiced craft of clay, glaze and fire

that gives contour to habits of dawn coffee
dusk Cap, to whatever desire I will pour.

It draws the outline to a small universe
already there. My palms know it.

The Highest Ranking at Lundy's
By Jennie Dear

Tuesday, 5:45 p.m.

"Writing the Great American Novel?"

Bernard had been reading over the woman's shoulder because he and his espresso and croissant were crowded into a corner of the coffee bar next to her, and because he was bored and because work had been crazy. Besides, there was nowhere else to look.

She didn't look up from her laptop. "Writing a Letter." The *L* was definitely capitalized. "You might be interested to know that after my last letter—to United Airlines about a canceled flight—the customer received a full refund, plus free round-trip airfare for a flight to anywhere in the domestic U.S."

Brown eyes, he noticed. "That's impressive. From the airlines."

"I get full results eighty percent of the time. That's why I've got the highest ranking at Lundy's."

"Lundy's?"

She looked at him as if he were impossibly slow, and absent-mindedly broke off a piece of his croissant. "That's the letter-writing company."

"I didn't know people still wrote letters. Not most people, right?"

"You get letters from your bank and insurance company, don't you? And your college, or didn't you go?"

He nodded, ignoring the implied insult. She'd moved his plate closer and was attacking the croissant. It had been one of those days: The world had felt out of focus and obscure. She seemed clear and purposeful. "I mostly throw all that stuff out."

"Anyway, Lundy's offers traditional letters, emails, texts, short videos—whatever people need. To communicate. The love letters, those are actual letters most of the time. But I've done them as texts, too." She smiled to herself as if remembering something.

"My name's Bernard, by the way."

She paused as if giving her name might be too intimate. "Rosemarie."

"How much would something like that cost—like, say, a complaint letter to an airline?"

"Are you interested in using our services?"

"I can take care of my own texts and emails. But thanks."

Her eyes narrowed briefly in disapproval. "Our average client pays $10,000."

He whistled, and several customers glanced up from their coffees and cell phones. "Sure you're not working for some kind of drug ring?"

She turned off the laptop and snapped its lid shut.

He hadn't been at his best earlier, was still distressed by the bird illustration he was working on, with an awkward neck he couldn't seem to fix. But he shouldn't have said he tossed out letters he received, or he shouldn't have said it that way. And he probably shouldn't have made a joke about a drug ring, for that matter, although what she was saying didn't seem to be making much sense. "You've got customers who'll slap down $10,000 for a letter?"

She had one arm in her jacket sleeve, getting ready to go, but she paused a moment with that exasperated look. "It's a lot more complicated than that, but most people do find the letters are worth more—much more—than they initially believed."

Her lips pressed together in a thin line. "Anyway, that's not how it works. A person comes in and pays, say, $50, or maybe even $15 or $20, if it's for just a few texts. After we've composed several communications for them, we begin building a relationship. It doesn't take them long to realize how much we have to offer." She stopped for a sip of coffee and more of his pastry.

Bernard said nothing. She reminded him of a girl in second grade, a kid who held the other children spellbound with her storytelling through recess or entire lunch periods. They would gladly have deserted their games and squabbles for her stories every day. What had her name been?

Rosemarie continued: "That's just for the personal communications. Our business clients are already on board when they come to us. You heard about the Barkley and Ponce merger?"

Bernard was impressed despite himself. "You played a role in that?" He thought a moment. "But how could Lundy's be sure…"

"That our letter was responsible? Ad tracking has come a long way, you know."

He did know.

"Anyway, my bosses have me do some of the corporate work because my results are consistently better than anyone else's, but I'm much more interested in the psychology on a personal level. Of course, it's all on a personal level. That's why Lundy's is successful. Because we get that." She popped the last bite of croissant into her mouth and stood up.

She slid a free magazine toward him. "Here's something to keep you entertained. Because I have to leave now."

She disappeared out into the street, and Bernard thought that while she'd been a bit snippy, he didn't care because for a half hour, the hamster wheel in his brain had stopped spinning in circles and he'd been thinking instead about something interesting and uncommon. And slightly mysterious.

8:00 p.m.

At home, he searched *Lundy's:* an island in the British channel, the governor of Londonderry, a New Zealand murder victim, a fiddler—and, "Letter writers to the world." He clicked on the link and the site began slowly loading.

At work, Pete gave him grief for spending too much time perfecting an image—*It's just a logo, for crying out loud*—so Bernard brought his projects home. When he had an illustration right, it didn't mean the image was flawless. It wasn't. But it gave him a feeling of completeness.

He could always tell from customers' faces when an ad fit what they'd been seeking, when it rose beyond mere fulfillment of a commercial order to something more gratifying. Even if it was only a logo.

Like everybody else, his company was driven more and more by clicks per view and time on a page, and he didn't even know what other quantifiables determined the styles and images and effects the illustrators were supposed to produce.

He glanced back at the Lundy's web page, where elaborately carved gold scrolls were materializing on the sides of the page, and, next to them, heavy theater curtains—deep crimson—and the colors on the page were luxuriant, echoing the vibrant inks in illustrated manuscripts. Now, a glossy black figure with glints of silver and brass was emerging between the curtains and he realized it was an ancient, but apparently functional, Underwood typewriter.

Bernard's first impulse was to laugh. The machines were particularly useless antiques—he'd tried using one and couldn't get over the snail's pace or the difficulty in correcting typos or switching paragraphs—but whoever had photographed this one was an artist. The light was soft, gleaming on the type hammers and carriage release lever, transforming the contraption into an object of inscrutable wonder.

Saturday, 11:30 a.m.

The coffee bar was crowded again, but he figured he'd drink his espresso standing up. Another woman, Rosemarie-like, had spread her things across three places at the counter. As he walked by, she spoke without turning around: "Yes to another coffee, in case you're offering."

Rosemarie, of course, but she seemed even smaller than before, dressed in black—a scarf, a loose sweater, and a skirt—and sitting with legs tucked underneath her on the stool.

Bernard paid the three extra dollars for another double espresso, and while he was at it, two croissants. He sat down next to her, moving her papers over to clear a space for the food and coffee. "Working on another letter to the airlines?"

Her fingers made brisk, punching sounds on the laptop's keyboard as she typed. After a few minutes, she hit send, and only then did she turn to answer him. "Letter for a man who just got sent back to Mexico. He lived in the States for fifteen years."

She either hadn't slept, or if she had, she'd tried to do it here, at the coffee bar. She was delicately demolishing her croissant, so he pushed the second one toward her.

"Lucky for him, your letters are eighty percent effective—isn't that what you said?" He'd meant it as reassurance, but maybe it hadn't come out that way.

"Hernando thinks they might go after his wife too. She and the kids are in hiding. One of them's only three years old—does that seem like justice to you?"

Furious and desperate, and maybe on the brink of tears. Getting too close to the client must be one of the potential hazards of her job, he thought. He watched as she finished the first croissant and half of the second. "Do you ever write more than one letter for the same person? Like, say, if the first airlines refund letter had been unsuccessful, would you write a second?"

"Policy is, if you get absolutely no results after one letter, we'll compose up to two more at no extra cost. If you get a response with some results but not the result as per your request—say you wanted a full refund plus the costs of your overnight hotel, and the airline agreed to pay just your ticket refund—then we'll compose up to an additional two communications at a fifty percent discount."

"So maybe you could write more letters for the guy in Mexico?"

"Already did. I can do one more. Just not right now." She gave a last sad look at her computer screen, and then powered it off. "I'm going for a walk—want to come?"

The espresso and both croissants were gone, and he'd been trying to escape a dingy Saturday morning feeling. "Sure."

They rose to leave, and an older couple nabbed their seats at the counter before they'd even reached the sidewalk and started heading toward Central Park.

Rosemarie brushed something from the side of her face with her hand. He should try to cheer her up. "Tell me something else you're working on."

She cleared her throat. "Nothing much—mostly disinvites."

He looked at her blankly.

"Say you've invited someone to your wedding, but they're going through a horrible divorce. Do you still want both the husband *and* the wife at your wedding? But how do you approach the problem diplomatically?"

Bernard had not given much thought to weddings, let alone invitation lists. But he could see her point. "I don't know. What would you write?"

She raised an eyebrow. "It always depends on the personalities involved. You can read what I've got so far." She pulled a letter out of her pocket, and he smiled to himself. She took her work home after hours too.

Dear Samantha,

Do you remember that time when we were kids—was it your idea?—when we sewed the openings shut in the boys' clothes while they were asleep, so they wouldn't be able to put their arms through their shirts or get their pants on? We thought we were so clever—

And do you remember, Dan ripped a new shirt (how were we supposed to know it was a good shirt?), and then they were all mad at us for the rest of the trip. But I'd do it all over again if I had the chance. Wouldn't you?

He wondered if she'd given him the wrong letter. "I don't see anything about disinviting Samantha. Or about a wedding."

Rosemarie didn't quite roll her eyes. "Look, this is a very delicate situation. You have to help the letter recipient recall connections and shared memories, and then build on those before you deliver the zing. You've got to consider long-term family relations, and the ripples."

Zing. Ripples. Bernard remained quiet.

"People observe them all the time in nature, and they think nothing of it. If you toss a pebble in a pond, the water is affected where the pebble enters—there's a splash, right? But that entry point isn't the only part of the pond that's altered. The pebble causes ripples that travel all the way to shore, and they continue for a long time—minutes." Her fingers made tiny rippling movements in the air, as if she were playing the piano. "You can also think of it as being like a web. You pluck a strand here," she raised her hands and pinched her fingers together, "and the whole web shakes. People consider most of their actions as if they're decisions made in isolation, or, at most, choices that only affect a few others. But they're wrong: Every decision shakes the web or produces ripples."

The fact was, the letter excerpt Bernard had just read didn't remotely deal with the situation she'd described. But he wasn't the client, and Rosemarie had an appealing way of explaining anything. It reminded him again of the girl in second grade. Marsha.

They walked the entire circumference of the Jackie Kennedy reservoir, then headed south to the Literary Walk. They passed a severe-looking woman, gray-headed, who was sitting at an easel and painting one of the trees. Rosemarie studied the painting and gave a quick little nod before they walked on, as if to say it, or the artist—or both—had passed muster. Then she turned to Bernard and asked, "You're an artist too, right?"

He laughed. "*Graphic* artist, which is the same as saying not much of an artist at all."

She shook her head. "You're an artist, all right. You're probably just feeling thwarted."

Thwarted. It struck him as a word from another time. On the other hand, it fit. Why else had he been working on corporate logos until after midnight?

She asked how he'd decided to become a graphic artist, and he wasn't sure. Or maybe he was, because it hadn't really been a decision. He'd expected to end up more like the woman with the easel.

Later, long after they'd finished the walk and he'd returned to his apartment, he'd realize he learned almost nothing about her—Did she have any friends? Was she from New York, or did she come from someplace else? Was she single? Probably yes to that last one.

When they said good-bye, there was a half second when he could have asked to see her again—maybe even that night—and he would have, but he remembered the two projects he wanted to finish over the weekend and kept his mouth shut.

Sunday, 11:00 p.m.

He completed the logos, but he continued to work on the bird illustration, now a picture of a wild goose. He wanted to catch the split second in the midst of the bird's struggle with gravity, or the moment after it won the fight and left the river for the sky.

He finally put down his charcoal pencil and permitted himself another look at the Lundy's website. He began by hunting for a tab with "Contact Us" or "About," or even "Menu." There were no tabs.

When he hovered the cursor over any of the typewriter keys, the key would change from black to gold. He clicked on the A, but nothing happened. He tried a couple of other keys—still nothing. On a whim, he pressed the A, the shift key, and L down at the same time. It seemed pointless, but then he noticed, with a thrill, that another page was gradually beginning to load.

A densely beautiful script appeared at the top:

Letters of Abelard and Heloise, Letter I

He'd heard the names before, in a college literature course—a nun and a monk who fell in love? He tried other key combinations and found other letters: Martin Luther King Jr.'s Letter from Birmingham Jail, (shift, and then the M, L, and K keys) and Gandhi's letter to Hitler (G and H). He tried to return to the page with King's letter, and somehow hit K, O, and L instead. This brought him to a page titled:

Kinds of Letters

He scrolled through a long list: Aphrodisiacal, Congratulatory, Consolatory, Eleemosynary, Filial, Hospitality, Legal, Marital, Maternal.

Under each general category were subcategories: Letters for Breaking Up After He has an Affair; Letters for Breaking Up after You have an Affair; Letters for Breaking Up for No Good Reason. Or: Letters Upon the Occasion of Your Eldest Son's Graduation; Letters upon the Occasion of Your Eldest Daughter's Graduation. Letters for Hosts Welcoming Guests, Letters for Hosts Wishing Guests to Depart.

For a moment, the complexity of personal relationships and life events seemed to have a neat, rational arrangement. Almost elegant, he thought.

Monday, two weeks later, 6:00 p.m.

Rosemarie had dyed her hair auburn and was wearing a yellow shirt, red pants, and bright green sneakers. Dark half-moons rimmed her eyes, and she appeared painfully thin. Maybe she was an abuser.

He skipped the croissants altogether and bought a giant turkey sandwich with provolone cheese, cranberry sauce, and lettuce. "Hey. It's me, Bernard."

She glanced up, smiling slightly, then saw the sandwich and picked it up. Mid-bite, she said, "He didn't do it."

"Who didn't do what?"

She made a face and let out a sigh, as if he should have intuited the answer, as if this were more evidence of how molasses-slow his brain was. "The man I'm writing this letter for. He's been convicted of a nasty murder—you don't even want to know. It's not surprising the judge was a bit hasty, because who has any sympathy for a baby killer? But this guy isn't the murderer." She was dispatching the sandwich even faster than usual and started to choke on a bite.

Bernard passed her his glass of water. "That sandwich isn't going anywhere if you eat it slowly."

She nodded, and then finished his glass of water and the sandwich. Maybe next time he'd get her something that came in bite-sized portions. "How do you know he didn't do it?"

"I know."

He studied her. Maybe she did know. "Who'd you address the letter to?"

"One to the governor, one to the defense attorney, one to the judge."

"Any chance you're diluting your power?" Maybe he shouldn't have asked that, but then he saw her shift thoughtfully.

"I don't know. I think I told you, we don't typically write more than three letters to the same person. And we almost never write to multiple parties for the same client. But what else could I do?"

He shook his head.

She wiped the crumbs from the table in front of her. "Got to go, sorry. I have a corporate merger and a political situation going on—"

He gave her a pained look, and her face brightened a little: "Don't worry, it's a couple of tiny nations in the South Pacific. We're not talking World War III here."

Tuesday night, 8:00 p.m.

In his wild goose illustration, the bird's wings seemed to spread and flap furiously without being able to rise above the river.

The Lundy's site wasn't especially user-friendly, not for people who didn't have special instructions or codes. He couldn't determine any logic to its organization. Still, maybe he could find a staff list. He tried several possible combinations with the shift key: L and W (for Letter Writers), W and S (for Writing Staff), then different combinations with W. No luck.

He started to search under R, for Rosemarie, pairing it with different letters as he went through the alphabet. Then he skipped to R and J—a lot of last names began with J. When he typed in R and K, the combination finally took him to another web page:

Rosemarie Knight

In the center of the page was a thumbnail video with a black-and-white still. In the shot, maybe fifty or a hundred people were working in the grand reading room of a library. They sat at a series of wooden tables with tiny lamps, some of them using laptops, some writing on paper tablets, and two or three videoing themselves with their smart phones.

He pressed play.

The video began with a wider shot of the circular room: Towers of bookshelves came into view, ladders placed along bronze rails that ran the length of the shelves. The camera zoomed in on one of the workers, and he realized it was Rosemarie. She smiled directly at the camera then returned to typing on her computer. Someone approached her table, but he was only visible from the chest down. The stranger—it was a man—made a gesture, as if asking a question. There was no audio, but Bernard could see that Rosemarie asked a question in return and then sat and listened, her eyes alive with concern. After a few seconds, she nodded, arose, and walked down a long corridor and then disappeared into murky darkness.

It reminded Bernard of the early silent movies and their sense of mystery. He replayed the video several times, and then he turned to the rest of the page. On the left side was a bulleted list, starting with:

Effectiveness: 95% results; 80% full results.

Apparently, her letters were even more successful than she'd claimed. He continued reading:

Rates: By individual communication or by the hour. Add additional 40 percent to general rates.

After that, a boilerplate paragraph that began with:

As a writer for Lundy's, Ms. Knight provides efficient, effective results.

For her first three letters, results are guaranteed, or the Client will receive a full refund. After said first three letters, as long as the correspondence meets our listed effectiveness rate, no particular results are guaranteed.

Bernard skipped down to:

Specialties: Corporate, General, Gratitude, Hostage Crises, Personal Crises, Political Crises.

Occasional: Marriage proposals, Letters Announcing Divorces, Suicide Notes.

Jesus Christ, he thought.

Tuesday, two months later, 6:30 p.m.

Bernard had been visiting the coffee bar every Tuesday and Saturday, but Rosemarie hadn't been there until now, when he saw, with surprise and relief, that she was at her former spot at the counter.

She gave him a half-smile and pointed to an array of food in front of her. "Look, I bought us both dinner."

Two large salads, three sandwiches, and two espressos. Also, a thickly frosted piece of carrot cake and a slice of pie, purple juices leaking out from under its chestnut-colored crust.

"Looks like Thanksgiving."

She must have been expecting him, which made him feel both flattered and puzzled. He sat down and picked up a fork. "Thanks. It's good to see you." He placed the napkin in his lap, and then said, lightly, "Hey, I was looking at the Lundy's website, and it's a little…well, unusual, don't you think?"

She stared back at him coldly. "In what way?"

He could have mentioned the correspondence from the twelfth century, or the lack of even the most basic directions and information. He thought about the specialties attributed to Rosemarie, like hostage crisis letters; he couldn't imagine what sort of pressures she must be under. And he wondered about any political crises she might have been involved in, and at what level. But what he said was: "Please don't tell me you write suicide notes."

She nodded. "We help people express themselves well, clearly, artistically. Wherever they most need our services."

Bernard put his fork down. He hadn't taken a bite. "Wouldn't it be better to call 911? To get a counselor there? If you don't care about the ethics, you might at least concern yourself with possible legal consequences."

"Lundy's takes care of all of that—they call emergency services, sometimes they even pay for counseling. But if someone wants his final letter to the world to be well-written and eloquent, why would we deny him his dying wish?" She had somehow downed an entire sandwich, but her hand was trembling as she reached for a second.

He spoke more gently. "Didn't you say your bosses let you do what you wanted, mostly—can't you ask them to stop assigning you suicides and wrongfully convicted prisoners and immigrants who are being dragged back across the border without their families? Whatever happened to complaints to the airlines and disinvites?"

She shook her head. "What if I did that—if I gave those cases to somebody else, and then something happened to one of them? How am I supposed to live with that?"

"What happened to the Mexican guy?"

She relaxed slightly. "I think that's going to work out. I talked to my supervisors, and we arranged to write letters from Hernando's children."

She took a bite of salad. "So, I wrote to their Congressional representatives—those letters were given immediate attention, especially the one from the five-year-old. No actions yet, but I think something's in the works."

"Congratulations." Bernard decided he didn't need to eat anyway. She could probably stand to take home a doggy bag. "Any luck with the guy on death row?"

She pushed the remains of the salad away and dug into the cake, chewing slowly, and swallowing before answering. "The execution's been scheduled."

October through February

Every couple of weeks, she would be there, at the coffee bar. Each time, the dark circles under her eyes had deepened and she seemed skinnier.

Once, he spotted her at the Museum of the City of New York. He shouldn't have been surprised: Rare Thomas Jefferson letters were being showcased in a special exhibit.

She was upset, and this time, Bernard knew why. He'd started watching the progress of the prisoner's appeal, with the back and forth between the courts and the defense lawyers. The Supreme Court had refused to hear it.

"I heard the statement from the governor in Texas about your prisoner yesterday. He sounds pretty adamant."

She nodded. "I have one more strategy. I'm writing a letter from a witness who didn't come forward originally, and I'm going to the press. It's his only hope."

She didn't look hopeful, Bernard thought. She looked gaunt and angular and wretched. But he couldn't think of anything to say or do, so he wished her luck.

Another time, at the coffee bar, she was crumpled into a ball in one of the leather club chairs. He reached down to touch her forehead and she didn't move. He was late for work, but before turning to leave, he slipped a couple of twenty-dollar bills under her purse.

She unfolded herself. "Lundy's pays me very well."

"How well?"

She sat up. "Six figures. Part of it's based on commissions, of course, but those have never been an issue."

Money wasn't what she needed, anyway. "Is there anything I can do?"

She shook her head. "But you'll be glad to know, I told Lundy's no more suicide notes."

Saturday, a month later, 11:30 a.m.

It was rainy and gray, and Bernard slept in, but as soon as he began looking at headlines, he saw it. A small story near the bottom of the web page, black letters stark against the white of the computer screen: Texas prisoner executed.

He checked the Lundy's website, and clicked on R and K, but the letters didn't take him to Rosemarie's page. Maybe she'd been fired, or maybe she'd quit. Or maybe she'd been transferred to a less stressful position.

The rain was coming down more heavily now and by the time he arrived at the coffee bar, he was soaked. Inside, the place was warm and steamy, buzzing with conversations and the roar of the espresso maker. Rosemarie wasn't at the counter or the corner table or in the leather chair.

He stayed to drink his espresso, and then another. He bought himself two sandwiches in her honor. Then the weather began clearing up, and he suddenly didn't want to be at the coffee bar any longer. He left the second sandwich on the counter—just in case.

He retraced the route he'd taken with Rosemarie months ago. When he arrived at the spot where the severe-looking artist had been working, he saw only her easel and an empty folding chair. She must have run into a café when the rain started.

He sat down in the chair and then stood quickly because a puddle had formed in the rounded wood seat. The artist had left a metal box of materials behind her chair, and he pulled out an art tablet and placed a blank sheet on the backboard. Her box of paints held watercolors—not his favorite medium—but he wet a brush and began.

It had been a long time since he'd used paints at all, so he worked painstakingly at first, and then with growing confidence, sticking to grays and blacks with streaks of blue. When he finished, he carefully ripped out the painting—a wild goose floating on a river—and placed it on his coat on the ground. He started another, this time a picture of a goose lifting off into flight.

He was painting faster now, his hand surer, and he completed the second painting, ripped the paper from the tablet, and began a third.

Some part of his mind noticed the sky had cleared completely, the spring sun felt warm, people had come out to play softball. The same part of his brain recognized the occasional crack of a bat hitting a ball and cheering, and children laughing and running as they returned to the park. Later, he heard the lonely notes of the children and parents calling to each other, leaving for the day as the light drifted and dimmed.

But even when the sun set and the air turned chilly, the artist hadn't returned to retrieve her easel and Bernard had forgotten it was someone else, not he, who had been standing at the easel in the park every day, that the paints and brush and easel didn't even belong to him, and he was still painting geese flying from the river, each bird more detailed, more exquisite, and each a little higher in the sky.

Chambers
By Sophia Zhao

Of liquid bone, she sips from empty glasses
brimmed with the cool ether of porcelain.
Many times it just tastes better with a
spoonful of sugar—after rainy nights, when

heaving exhausts curl through
the paper-thin windows. As if breathing in,
searching for a body through cement floors:
     so cold, so cold.

    A body; the sweetner;

why her eyes spoil and blacken, searing
a solidity lost from boiling decades
fed to the drain. It's been years since

she's burned herself, since she's left the
lip of steel kettles vying for a taste of
totality that spills some.
  She remembers, each morning

its ringing knuckle knock
against her pinewood bureau, a
sound so loud and still melded

into silent pulses of freefall
  —somehow, she never caught it.
Maybe, it's because of her palm stitched
from overlaps of expectancy;

for the door to unlatch its copper joints,
to undo her frame surrendered to

stillness. Stuck and she waits for
particles to form something substantive.

      Outside, the sky spits warmth and
forms a vessel. Limestone walls are
unpartitioning. Her hand

searches for a spoon, but it's
rusty. The room looks so sour.
Her throat churns to save

something famished.
Saliva looks like a pill
      , nothing is more filling.

Selected Poems by Jerrice J. Baptiste

Sacred moment

Forgetting the newly diagnosed disease

with a glimpse of a boy in a moving car

waving both cashew-colored hands,

sticking out tongue, then smiling.

Do You Smell That?

A veil of fragrance covers my face.
And its in mauve, in rose, in blows
of the wind. When I was a young girl

of thirteen, I wanted to know more
about the top-heavy flowers that leaned.
Easter Sunday, my nose craved
the scent of Hyacinth. A fancy name
like that, it better be
able to stand up straight, but no. After rain,

rain dances in Cilia's garden,
our neighbor whose lap I curled on
when thieves grabbed my gold chain

from behind my neck. In her small garden, we sat

sipping watermelon juice and inhaling
what nature has so freely given each season
I'm consoled by its bulbs.

Drumbeat
By Ingrid L. Taylor

How the crickets chant through the dark-spun trees on this night of heat and fog. Under a sand-washed sky of distorted constellations, I mistake Andromeda for Orion—a blooded hunter imbrued with the body of a queen. The wings of the crickets cut the particle-ridden sky, they scrape the night down to its bone char clarity & I know you, too, are awake, breathing in the stars. The alary chorus fills my lungs, oxygen exchanged for pitch and timbre. Beating against the firmament,

beating below me where chain link ribbons into dirt & becomes a discarded galaxy. I recall the cuttlefish—how he sleeps under a billion starred sea, where eons before a pulsar folded to create something new. I cannot mark the time between how one star eats another or dreams furl inside this nocturnal churning. How the crickets' pulse answers my wild seething & I wish for two lives— the one I have & the one where I dive into the sea of sound

to escape my heart's red beating.
Trade my blood for hemolymph.
Raise my wings to friction.
Tremble my thighs to hardened
shield & welcome a tender
abdomen, an unchambered heart.
Resound to the arcing skyline a
cadence elevated on smoke and
starlight. A staccato winging
across the miles to tell you I want
to hold you again, skin to skin,
beneath a thrumming sky. To
drumbeat under your window on
this night of heat and fog.

A Lily on the Ward
By Cloe Watson

There is a woman lying
on the other side of the curtain,
a carousel of white foxes circling
above her mouth, her fine hair
binding itself into silver knots
as her head turns from right
to left. The body repeats
as the night bundles into the starless
burrows of madness, and a violet horse
leads the way to the shaded doorways
of each burrow, where I hover in turn,
wondering in which to place
the spinning Lily in my palm.

I wake—the yellow pill
has had its time within me,
its dissolving, the savior
of a tardy sleep. How
did I get from bed to this circle
of chairs, to this *Smile Club?*
The woman standing in front
says *boundaries* over and over
in between other smaller words
as the girl next to me inches
her chair closer to mine,
each metallic squeak, a tickle
to my muffled ears. I'm flattered,
despite her blonde hair—curdled
in indignity. The cigarette burns
on the back of her hand

look like the spotted moon
I once loved, and I wonder
if I should show her my Lily,
my hands picking through my pocket,
hardly knowing it has been placed
somewhere deeper than that.

Mourning in the Metaverse
By Dion Farquhar

I sit slouched in my old Audi, rain pounding

the windshield, heater humming

Vivaldi's *Gloria* roaring on the CD

waiting for my life partner (the current term)

    the one I left my city for

    my *one really good choice*

to get out of PT (gait and balance training)

his lymphoma diagnosis new last month

aggressive chemo looming (despite co-morbidities)

but the jubilation on the soundtrack

can't stanch this bonfire

    sparked by the absence of adult sons

    first Christmas without them

    thriving in distant parts of the country

    (happier—and smarter—than most at their age)

    feasting with partners' kin

dispiriting dread, denial's diminishing power

widow a new identity category looming

ghost parade of family and friends

      even acquaintances extinguished

places vaporized, malled and gentrified, meadows paved over

recipes lost (no middle-class inheritance, furniture or china)

the slow, kindled, lingering death of the book

the university shrunk to job training

layers of personal and political collide

I may be out of sync

but never a cheery deer

credulous in the headlights

spurning "home space"—*whatever you find the most beautiful*

and what would *that* be for *my* avatar?

the lost youth, decades like batch files

what I *could* have done and *should* have known

the parents and past I needed to shed and forget

though much remembering needed

to forge consolation through slow cooking

spriteful love, sanguine labor

retrofitting recognition

no catch-up despite the shifting ground:

so many books forgotten, people dead

Kyle two years ago the day after Thanksgiving

a fatal heart attack on the toilet

and my Broadway went dark

no notice we all wouldn't go on forever

a little entropy here and there

and now, on another, very mid-morning day

with all these rememberings going on

I remembered I forgot

to offer the two friends over for Sunday brunch

the rugelach from Russ and Daughters

(raspberry, apricot, chocolate)

they'd have loved it

now my Sweetie's pushing

the heavy door of the PT place

I punch in the radio knob

spring out of the car

handicapped spot right in front

extend my arm, so he can lean on it

slowly, start walking together

toward the passenger door

look at each other, smile

Hi, how'd it go?

Losing Sienna
By Christina Roscoe

Names have been changed to honor privacy.

Sienna was all baby lamb, gangly and vulnerable on the ice. The straps on her equipment wrapped around twice, the manufacturer having failed to account for such delicate bones. After practice, we'd change: she into boys' undershirts and Adidas shorts, I into floral skorts. At ten, I had a mouthful of wire, octagonal glasses, and bangs like a five-year-old. Sienna had perfect teeth and vision. Her ivory-blond hair, perpetually uncombed, was nevertheless silken, hyper-clean. The roundness of my face was a constant torment to me, but Sienna had a face like a heart. She loved soccer and dogs. I loved my dolls and God. Still, an embarrassing deficit thrust us into shared orbit. We were the only girls on our 1995 Minneapolis ice hockey team who could skate but not stop. In this way, I met her— hurtling down the rink with no end game.

During our first carpool, Sienna said, "I can tell you anything you want to know about Pembroke Welsh Corgis, Cavalier King Charles Spaniels, Bernese Mountain Dogs and, like, dozens of others."

"Oh!" I said, alarmed. "Um . . . the mountain dogs, I guess?" On Sienna's carpool days, her mother used the McDonald's drive-through. I'd given up meat for Lent, an act too mortifying to share with these non-believers, and anyway, I could count on one hand the times I'd suffered fast food. While Sienna chewed, I cast about for a witty remark. Desperate, I apologized to Jesus for steamrolling Matthew 7:12—"Do unto others" and all that—and said: "Is it just me or does Coach seem like he's got a body or two in his basement?" Sienna choked so hard on her fries her mother had to pull over. Having decided I was funny, Sienna overlooked my breathtaking ignorance about everything that mattered to her: MTV, video games, the World Cup, and canines.

At first Sienna was a "hockey friend," reserved for winter months. But the summer I turned twelve, it occurred to me that *freedom* sat in our garage taking on rust. I called Sienna's house. "Can I bike over?" I asked, twisting our phone cord into an intractable helix.

"Sure," she said. "We don't have anything to eat though."

"Let's cook."

"Um, no. Can't use the stove," she reminded me. We microwaved marshmallows instead, shrieking as the candy melted through melamine.

The first time Sienna saw my bedroom, her gaze settled on my dolls. They occupied every corner—here asleep in cherrywood cradles; there, reclining in wicker rocking chairs; the rest in the corner, anticipating tea. Sienna's bedroom was plastered with soccer posters and contained exactly no dolls. "What's in the storage trunk?" she asked. This question made me nervous.

"My doll clothes," I admitted and, afraid she would lift the lid to see for herself, added: "And formal invitations to tea parties, and my tea set. Doll books. Their winter boots and extra shoes, straw hats—stuff like that." Sienna was eternally skeptical, and her wit could leave a mark. She might have been cruel about my playthings. Instead, she grinned.

"You definitely need more dolls," she said.

One day, I biked over to find her mother locking up. "Hey! Want to come to a professional women's soccer game?" Sienna asked. Sitting on the metal bleachers, I licked the salt off my giant pretzel.

"Why don't they pass the basketball more?" I asked.

"They—wait. What?" she said.

"I thought basketball was all about passing," I said, feigning seriousness.

"You—but this is a . . . what?" She cocked her head and looked at me, unsure. *My God, it's too easy.* I erupted with glee. "You're such an idiot," she giggled, shoving my shoulder. After the game, I followed Sienna onto the field. Cast long, our shadows drew close, her fingers through mine if only on turf. Longing radiated down between my legs and clenched, leaving me wet and bewildered.

I noticed the light like never before. The cerulean sky, normally so evocative of Heaven, seemed irrelevant: a scrim behind the setting sun, obliterating and fierce. I turned to Sienna, and she turned to bronze. Her eyes in sun were the gray of my beloved agate, a depthless color no one else would ever see. Her lashes were longer than I knew, lit to the tips by that searing light. *I wish this day would never end.* Already, the wish felt like tragedy. In a moment of clarity, I realized I would never have enough Sienna.

The summer after seventh grade, Sienna's aunt took us fishing, and I—by then a button-wearing member of People for the Ethical Treatment of Animals and a strict vegetarian—reeled in one sunfish after another, stringing them up on twine. Sienna's laughter extracted from me such unbridled joy, it was like meeting myself for the first time. I was willing to forget who I was for her. In a mishap calculated to summon her laugh, I cast my hook in a tree. "You caught a branch, dummy!" she shouted.

"I'm not the first one!" I protested. "Someone's bobber is up there." Delighting in my predicament, we yanked together on the line. Sienna's pale arms moved against my tanned ones, electrifying the fishing pole.

In eighth grade, Sienna's father pulled up outside my school in his black Miata convertible. He rolled down Sienna's window and leaned over her, said *sotto voce,* "Hi, Christina."

"Hi, Jeffrey," I giggled. He was all camp, this gorgeous gay man.

"Ready for the tournament?" Jeffrey asked, batting his eyes.

"I guess," I said. For me, the "hockey" of it all had become secondary. I played for time with Sienna.

He stretched out a bag. "Twizzlers?"

"No, thank you," I said, settling in.

"Oh, don't be so polite, Ms. Thing," he said. "I can't eat this whole bag. Take some." He thrust it in my face, and I pinched off a strand of strawberry pull 'n' peel. I noticed the bright "FAT-FREE" banner across the package. My body relaxed into that expanse of new leather and my pulse took a stroll. I was so happy to be warm, with the girl I loved and a whole bag of fat-free sugar.

Finished with my licorice, I unzipped my maroon Jansport backpack. "I brought something, too," I said, pulling out a bag of red foil-wrapped hearts. Sienna turned around to look. Her eyebrows lifted.

"Ooh, chocolate!" she said happily.

"Keep those away from me," Jeffrey said. "I'll get fat."

"Oh please," I said, "you'll never get fat." He rolled his eyes. "Happy Valentine's Day!" I managed, handing the bag up to Sienna. There was spectacular hope coiled in this gesture. *Seventeen* magazine, which circulated in art class, insisted today was the day to tell that special someone how you feel . . . with chocolate!

In my daydreams, Sienna's hand would brush my own. "Happy Valentine's Day," she would say, uncertain, looking at me hard. We'd be in the back seat of her father's car, "Dancing Queen" playing so loud up front that we'd be alone with our words. "Huh," Sienna would say. "Hearts."

"Did you get any other valentines today?" I'd ask.

"Is this supposed to be a valentine?" she'd say. I'd nod my head and brave a shy smile.

"No," she'd say. "Not like this."

"Not from a girl, you mean?"

"Not from someone I actually like," she'd say, and my face would flush hot. I'd seek out the imperfection in her green-gray iris, that tiny dark fleck I adored, so sure it was known only to me. Emboldened, I would lean in, but hesitate. Then she would kiss me so fiercely our teeth would clash. I would press her against the seat and straddle her, knees digging into leather as I ran my tongue along her neck, her collarbone.

In real life, Sienna took the chocolate and smiled. "Thanks! Want some?"

"Nah," I said. I was already full, bones to skin, by a wrenching desire to put my lips on her mouth, her breasts, her stomach, and lower.

That spring, the smell of Sienna haunted my dreams and made my stomach quiver, made me want to tear my hair out. There was no one to tell, no way to bottle it up, no way to have her in the way that I wanted her, ever. No way to make myself right. One day I suggested we surprise her mother and clean the house. This was a compulsion of mine, gratifying grownups. In this way I was cursed. Trudging upstairs with a pile of clean shirts, I suddenly understood. Sienna smelled like her laundry detergent. "What detergent do you use?" I called down, casually.

"My mom does my laundry," she yelled. "It's probably Tide." *It isn't Tide. We use Tide. When I'm not with you I can't find you anywhere.* Down in her basement, I found what I was looking for: a bottle of Downy.

"Why don't we buy Downy?" I asked my mom that night.

"What's wrong with Tide?" she asked, confused.

"I love her," I wanted to say. "It's the closest I'll ever come to having her," I wanted to say.

"Nothing," I said.

At thirteen, I joined Sienna's family on vacation. Jeffrey took us to the movies to see "My Best Friend's Wedding." Rupert Everett played the first openly gay character I'd encountered—on screen or onstage. It was at once exhilarating and unimaginable. We passed the popcorn and howled with laughter. Suddenly Sienna— filled with the jubilance of the moment—turned and planted a kiss on my cheek. In the darkness, a flight of horses wilded across my heart. *Does she want to . . .? Would she ever . . .?* Exiting the theater, I walked into a garbage can, dazed. I should ask her if she's kissed anyone. Tonight. After we've turned out the lights. I should say, "Let's just practice on each other."

Back at the rental cottage, I stared at the lake. I tried to appear lost in thought, waiting for Sienna to ask what I was thinking about. The answer was, of course, *her*. Truth turned to tiger beneath my ribs, pacing, crazed. Sienna spun in her swing, toeing a circle in the sand. Finally, I said, "Should we play that game where we guess what the other person is thinking?"

She shrugged. "Nah," she said.

In ninth grade, I went to the library as often as possible to test my gayness. I'd take a non-linear route to the barely-there section on "Homosexuals and Homosexuality." I used a decoy book, wide and tall, to hide whatever queer thing I was reading. *Being Homosexual: Gay Men and Their Development* had no answers for a fourteen-year-old girl. *Beyond Acceptance: Parents of Lesbians and Gays Talk About Their Experiences* opened with parents explaining that, when their child came out, they considered mutual suicide. This only confirmed my fears. But the book I returned to, again and again, contained the Kinsey scale and a test to determine one's sexual orientation:

"Question 1: To whom are you attracted?"

Well. Cole from Spanish class. He's gay but he still counts. I think he counts. Does he count? Either way. Sienna. Liza, I guess.

Chloé on that Boundary Waters canoe trip . . . gosh, that was brutal.
I selected "mostly people of the same sex as mine."

"Question 2: Who have you had sex with?"

Um. Next.

"Question 3: Who have you had sexual fantasies about?"

Sienna. Matt Damon, when he breaks down in "Good Will Hunting." Sienna. Angelina Jolie in "Gia." Sienna. The guy in "Ordinary People" who tries to off himself. Sienna.

The Kinsey test didn't work on me. It couldn't tell what I was. I usually got a "3," which meant I was equally heterosexual and homosexual. Some days I got a "2," some days a "4." None of it was helpful. I wanted to know whether this terrible condition was reversible. I wanted to know whether lesbians could ever be happy.

By the tenth grade, I had three new coaches. As far as I knew, these were the first queer women I'd ever met. The new assistant coaches moved through the world like the men I knew: reserved, hands thrust deep in their pockets. The new coach, too, kept her own counsel. She wore heavy work boots and drove a pickup truck. It was clear, based on all available evidence, that people like me grew up to be butch. This was a bleak discovery. I couldn't find myself anywhere in my coaches. I scavenged for similarities, came up empty, and wept with rage. I imagined my adulthood and vomited, great waves of self-hate, despair. *I don't want to coach hockey or drive a truck.* Still, I couldn't bear to be this lonely for the rest of my life. *What is the point of growing up, only to be alone?*

On Christmas Eve, I stopped by Sienna's house. We were losing the light. The sky looked like *melancholy* rendered in watercolors. Sienna's couch smelled like dog fur. Sienna smelled like Sienna, like everything I'd ever wanted. Sienna paged through her favorite dog training manual.

I had a plan, but broad strokes, without detail. "My mom and I are fighting," I finally said. It wasn't true, this, but I didn't know how else to begin.

"Uh huh," she said.

"She wants to know why I don't have a boyfriend," I said. By now my heart was riotous in my throat. "I want to tell her, like, Mom, I'm never gonna have a boyfriend, okay? I'm attracted to girls." Sienna looked up.

"You . . . what?" she said.

"Yeah," I said, exhaling with a weariness that transcended our years: "I like girls."

"Oh. Wow," she said. She looked confused, like she didn't know if she'd heard right. "Really?" she said again, after a long silence. I saw her tumbling thoughts, the question at the center of it all. I longed to answer and say I was terribly, desperately in love with her. I wished I could tell her she was my sun, that my waking hours were an orbit in her honor. That I was tormented by her smell, agonized by the thought that I would never, ever, have her. That she had replaced hunger, thirst, and fatigue, leaving me with nothing but a giant Sienna-shaped hole. That she was everywhere at once, and nowhere near enough.

"I like girls," I repeated. I was suddenly exhausted. I felt the crushing weight of my own homophobia only as it lifted. The feeling of release was so real that I turned to look behind me, but there was only sky—that giant canvas without hope.

"Can I tell my dad?" she asked. Jeffrey, whom I adored, was the only gay man I knew.

"Yeah, okay," I said, "but no one else." Sienna smoothed the manual's cover in a repetitive circular motion. I worried the cuff of my khakis. Finally, a car pulled up outside: my parents, come to take me to church.

"Hey," she said as I rose to go.

"Yeah?" I said.

"Thanks for telling me," she said.

"Yeah," I said. In that instant, I saw that she had understood everything, mistaken nothing. For the first time in my adolescence, I was un-erased. If only one person knew, well, one was more than none.

On Christmas morning, though, I awoke with a terrible realization. Sienna had not said she liked girls. In this gentle way, she had rejected me. The shame that quit me with ferocity on Christmas Eve surged back with equal violence. I became self-conscious in the locker room. *Does she think I'm watching her undress?* Our conversations in the car became stilted, or maybe I was projecting. We—I—had lost the levity from before I came out, an act so serious and irreversible that, in that time and place, it changed everything. It struck me that I had killed something we loved. When the season ended, I was too ashamed to call her. *What will I even say?*

Or maybe it was Sienna who fled, moving on to soccer, to friends who were not drowning in lust for her.

Maybe there was just nothing left to hold on to. The joy I felt when we were together emanated from that truest hope: that Sienna might love me, too. Without any hope, I couldn't find joy.

Maybe all of these things were true. Maybe none of them were. Or maybe I lost Sienna because she did not love me back—nothing more, and nothing less. Just enough to lose her.

Vibrations
By Vivian Holland

I like to think of you
and I as waveforms ebbing

and flowing through life,
smoothed out heartbeats

or humming violin strings rocking
air particles, tides

licking toes painted silver
and lavender, high-arching hues

that cut through the atmosphere
breathlessly—we

mighty photons,
we coaster tracks stretching for miles

might crest ever higher
if we were to interfere.

Selected Poems by Isabel Mader

August

We have been eating only wild blueberries
They grow in every bend of the bank
where the turtles lay like polished stones
small eyes gleaming, red-ringed

Our sons' tongues, hands are dark, sticky viscous
like gore in the corners of their sharp-toothed mouths
This is the only place I get to see the version of you
I used to know. The one you say is dead

buried beneath the hemlock tree
I ask you, drying dishes, *Is he here yet?*
You cup my face in stained hands. *Not yet.*
Our sons' fingers pluck, rake the fat gems from the bushes

Next week, the season will be over. They seem to know
Plunging their fists into the deep, they gorge like bears do
like the blue-muzzled fawn I saw this morning
like the mallards with their berry-dyed feet

There is not much time left. We are waiting for you,
all sun-warmed flesh, urgency.

Mothering

It is July again. The blue jay's corpse
lying beneath the oak tree, a shard of sky
he is still-feathered and stiff

Our sons peer into the yawning socket
of his eye, not seeing. I am sick
with something I cannot name

The permeability of my heart
How much of this do I owe to time
pooling like beads of water on gold

This morning, an ant crawled into the blue jay's open beak
and did not crawl back out
Just between us, I fear I am still hollow.

It's Been Years
By K. Degala-Paraíso

A golden shovel after Mary Oliver

mere minutes after i got the call that i never expected to receive i
began to Look / for any sign that you were still somehow alive
somehow here just hiding in a different form maybe in The / garden
as a yellow tulip or as a butterfly whose close encounter is just a little
too close to be random or speckled sunshine bearing down through
the Trees / i was so sure that i would recognize you as you now Are /
i promise i've been looking so hard to find you Turning / the slightest
movement in the corner of my eye every gasp of wind every newborn
baby as they open Their / little hands i almost vomit up my heart every
time expecting to see you emerge in their uncurling fingers stretching
your Own / arms to the sky like *hallelujah to have been gifted multiple*
Bodies / *hallelujah praise the generous lord* except their little hands
are always bare always empty it turns out that even a perfect morsel
of human goodness doesn't have enough magic to metamorphose the
dead Into / some kind of something so that i may place you atop altars
mantels bookshelves podiums spice racks Pillars / anything
everywhere cover this planet with the memory of you so that the
whole world might know some kind Of / new Light /

Editor
By Maxwell Griego

Phrases filtered obsessively
searching for strength
and specificity
and symbolism.

Words so saturated
in thought
that they become
too drenched to
stick to the page.

Soil Amendment
By Charissa Roberson

Based on the legend of Green Park, in London, England

I know you bring them flowers.

Lilies, dew-brushed white petals streaked with magenta, their straw-like stalks still milky with sap. Baby's breath, floating like cotton clouds on a balmy spring dawn. Dozens of roses, but special ones: pink petals trimmed with yellow, or yellow petals trimmed with pink. Columbine. Spiderwort. Daisies. Mums. Or, worst of all, those tiny purple wildflowers that everyone overlooks, but that I told you were my favorite.

I laid that garden myself. I tended it every morning and evening, watering the beds with care, cutting back the excess, turning the dirt with bare, soiled hands. I straightened stems with wooden skewers and bits of twine. I plucked out every weed, no matter how small, with ragged nails rimmed in dirt. And can you imagine? I thought of you.

Soiled.

When I was a child, I thought that was a nice word. A humble descriptor, for someone like me, who knelt in the garden and turned the dirt with her hands and breathed in the moist, clinging scent of earth heated by the sun.

But now I know. You are soiled, but not nicely, and the dirt under your fingernails is not hard work, but treachery.

Did you know me so poorly that you thought I would miss a single broken stem, a single missing bloom among my verdant children? I know when you plucked them from their life veins, when you forced them into beautiful arrangements, when you tied them together with stolen twine. I know when you fashioned a bouquet that wasn't meant for me.

I caught you at it, once: hands soiled in the midst of adultery. You hid the flowers behind your back, as if, at first, you believed me blind. Then you smiled—false gleaming of teeth!—and brought them out, already drooping from your sweaty fingers gripping too tight. You gave the bunch to me, like you'd planned it all along. And I accepted it. Sweet skies, I accepted it.

Maybe I still believed that old tale—how a dying rose spells the end of a curse, if only the girl can love a monster, just a little longer, a little longer.

I kept tending that garden, even knowing what I did. I saw the tread of your boots, pacing my carefully cultivated rows; I saw the imprint of your fingers, bending a stem until it snapped; I saw the smooth slink of your car, pulling in long past when your friends had turned for home. Yet I made those flowers bloom for you. I made their petals lush and fragrant. I made them turn toward you and smile as you cut off their heads.

When you left last night, hiding your dirty hands in the pockets of your coat, I knew you had a bunch of flowers wrapped inside that T-shirt. Who wouldn't? We move like actors in a farcical play, pretending not to see what's impossible to miss. We smile, and kiss, and circle on, while the audience—if there were one—would be striking their foreheads.

When you were gone, I went to my garden and sat by the bush I planted when I was sixteen. It has sharp branches, covered with thorns, and the buds are small. You'd never picked from it. It wasn't tempting enough. If you'd tried, you would've pricked your fingers, your tender, soiled fingers, and the prize wouldn't even be worth it.

As I sat amidst the branches, thorns pressed into my back, my shoulders, my skin. I tilted my head and saw the moon, patchworked with craters, arching over this silent half of the world. The moon does not see like the sun sees. The moon wears a blindfold, and it turns its darkest side to the void of space.

When you return tonight, with some excuse for your lateness that no one would buy, I won't unlock the door. I won't get up from the armchair and turn off my lamp, giving you the attention that you never deserved. I won't even roll those few inches aside so you can climb in beside me and soil our bedsheets with your lies.

There are stories they tell, of mothers who slit their own children's throats, rather than leave them to a fate worse than death.

Maybe they, too, did the deed by the light of an unseeing moon, thorns pressing into their flesh.

I took them with me, you see. All my fragrant, flowering children. Straggling roots still choke the ground, but they will never grow again.

The garden is empty now.

Will your charming smile—your smooth hands, your honeyed voice—be enough? Or could you only perform your treachery with my assistance; was it my fragrance, my loyalty, my beauty that let you work your wiles; and will you, too, start to wither when I'm gone, my turgor the only thing keeping you upright?

perennial
By Alisha Wong

by the time you are eighteen
i have watched you hope.
the trees have unstitched from moss.
and the clouds drink their dew.
the wind furls into your pocket as
you tuck your cigarettes inside wisteria.
your mother would be disappointed,
i tell you, hoisted on a branch,
twisting a bud between my fingertips.
you look up but don't reply,
and I grin as the backdrop falls.
later that day, i watch your words
fold into paper cranes as you tether
yourself to their flight.
your lungs make meat of your body—
an instrument of tendon and marrow.
your mother feeds you the pills
you can't keep down,
and you say it's like flying underwater.
the sun melts beneath sky
as crickets hum hymnal.
there is a white chrysanthemum
sprouting on your palm.
you say it's reparation for the wisps of hair
scattered across your sink.
the petals disintegrate and
i let them slip away until i knew you had
left the wisteria, until rain falls, until birds twitter,

until i knew your hope endured.
i should've stayed with you longer;
i remember a paper body stamped in blue,
sewn ashes over concave cavities.
we began forgetting feelings we knew
so you created the senses we long for,
but now there is nothing left to make,
      and i can no longer write of the first breath upon waking,
        the last breath before sleep,
          your bookmarks in my memory.

Selected Poems by Lexie Price

taking off a face

           her skin smooth and empty
           from this expanse
           of foundation, clearing the chaos.
           reaching her hand to gentle skin.
           manufactured solar
           brightness shadowing underneath
           her eyes, red-pink swirls of suns
           exploding across the lines of her cheeks,
           stars of glitter falling
           as she blinks.
     once. then,
     twice.

a wet cloth,
pulled from
plastic dark
as the night.
she takes her hand.
it doesn't
shake. she wipes away
the universe.

           the mirror steamed
           in the muted yellow
           bathroom light. hand reaching out
           to skin. the world
           beyond this   nebulous.

For Those Who Suffer Prophet Attacks

Once, in the haze of post-panic languid, I poeted prophecy to my best friend:

"The branches of the trees / are sketching / the sky."

> And he understood. I loved him for that.

I'd gone out from his house, from a simpler time, because the air inside smothered, and when I say I see it, I mean I see

—A mother / a child born / an early death / a first kiss like holiness / a scrape / a joy / a learning curve / a reason to die / no reason at all / a rock floating in space / we are *floating in space* / an inspection / a deflection / a trauma / that moment of being undeniably alone in a room full of people, the thing that hasn't happened yet, the thing that could *hurt us*—

I needed someone to believe me.

I've never felt grief like that which I hold for grieving Cassandra.

It is all of it right there in my head and it goes faster than anyone knows. Whipping wind. Tunnel vision. Chemical imbalance.

The world is very much. I can see it. My best friend came to see it with me.

I said it in the only way I could.

How to Live Alone
By Kira Santana

yet not feel lonely. or maybe you are. (it's okay to be.) make sure
that you locked the door three times before you leave your
apartment in the morning. get halfway down the stairs and run back
up again to check one more time—just to be safe. gaze into other
cars at red stop lights. look at the families off to school and work in
the mornings. the friends catching a ride. the girl with her windows
rolled down, listening to willie k and gripping the steering wheel
tightly with both hands. she is alone, like you. wonder if she
remembered to lock her door. if she has someone to come home to.
wish for a second that you could reach out, tell her it's okay. wish
you had someone to do the same for you. push away the thought.
compartmentalize it in the back of your mind, next to the wasted
friendships and the lost plans. spend the sunsets alone. take pictures
of the dwindling tangerine sorbet sky, but don't know who to send
them to. soak in the late night quiet. the moon bursting forth
between the palm trees outside your windows, the ocean's voice in
the distance, a low, yet forceful hum, company for even the loneliest
ones. shrink yourself one size too small. to fit into all of the places
you want to go, unnoticed, unburdening, so you won't need anyone
there with you. overdo it, yet still apologize for any space you do
take up. unlearn what it feels like to be wanted, to not feel like a
bother. live with the bellyache of an orange tree wound. of making
more food for dinner than you can eat alone and living off the
leftovers for days. of worrying in an aisle at the grocery store, if
you're buying too much, or not enough. wonder when your next
meal will be. dread splitting each recipe in halves, in quarters, for
just one, but it always ends up being more than you can eat. note
how a life alone feels like passing invisibly through liminal spaces.
how easy it is to fall (over) into rooms filled with nothing but dust.

step through each door on your tip toes, unsure if you ever belong. stop to smell the blushing hibiscus along kealaolu avenue. notice how every time you visit this street, it feels like you're seeing this island for the first time, heart launched into your left lung, the smell of petrichor wafting off the pavement after early morning showers, excitement settling in your stomach like sediment. the world seemed so vast then. now it feels small. but still beautiful. wrapped in the tendrils of your mind are thoughts of your family on the other side of the world. it's better not to miss them, so you try not to. miss them anyway. miss their incessant nagging, the home-cooked meals shared on weeknights, the mirage of a home in the moments where everyone seems to have a place in the house, a purpose, and life flows. get lost in the misplaced seasons, in how autumn never comes. walk the empty streets and think of no one. buy a lamp for your nightstand, watch the shadows cast themselves around your room, like friends surrounding you, as you huddle in the emanating light. whenever you are home, play music, or an audiobook, or leave the t.v. on, because you need the comfort of another human voice, and a distraction from your thoughts. watch the same shows you've seen dozens of times, because you don't have to fear the endings. refer to fictional characters in your head like your close friends. notice how the presence of the sounds of other people allows you to step away from yourself, and stand on the outside, away from the vicissitudes of growing within. quiet are dusty places. places where memories you don't let yourself think of have been laid to rest. like the smell of peonies, your mother's favorite flowers. or the cerise hue of lingonberry jam. or biking down a damp mountain trail with your brother. sit in a parking lot inside your car and text your online friends. tell them about how well you're handling being alone, about the hikes you've been on lately, walking below a forest canopy, breathing amongst hala and sandalwood trees. type yeah or lol when you don't know what to say, when you're afraid of saying the wrong thing, of losing them. ask your friends which dress they like better, the one in sky blue that reaches your knees, or the flowy beige one, that tickles the top of your ankles. wear the blue one, even when your online friends all agree on the latter, because it reminds you of the ocean. bring a book to the beach on sundays, so it feels like someone is there with you, with the shifting sands below and the words speaking from the page. tell the man who approaches you on the beach, who forces you to look up from your book to give him the light of day, that you have a boyfriend. that he's on his way and will be here soon. even though you are in your twenties, and no one is in love with you. you have practiced this lie before. invented a life for your make-believe lover. given him a name, a family, an address, even hobbies. make him sound so real that you can believe it yourself. so you seem confident, and unshaken. don't let him see that he has made you afraid. that you feel the most vulnerable when you are in a bikini, and his eyes feel like vultures, ripping up your skin with their sharp beaks. count your breaths down from ten as he walks away. pack up your things and try to calm your shaking hands. stand in the shower for an hour when you get home, trying to scrub the dirty feeling off. tell yourself you're safe, over and over again. feel yourself pass by the moon as driftwood. miniscule. invisible. a fleck of sea salt viewed through a 35mm lens. brew a cup of tea for yourself. sit in front of a computer and wait for the words to flow. tell yourself you should be writing, so write. pull your fingers down your face when the page remains blank. when every idea feels like a taunt, a reflection of your inadequacy, your loneliness. watch the cursor blink until the screen turns black. you need to write something. to not sit in this room alone. to at least live with the comfort of words around you, to be heard, even if it's just your own ears listening. hear the neighbor's dog down the hall, barking as someone walks past to the trash chute. wait for the sound of the door slamming, footsteps moving closer, then further away, the dog's voice fading into the background. stop listening because it hurts sometimes, to hear life so clearly in movement, to feel so stuck in the middle of it, unmoving, falling behind. fasten pictures of your friends, who are all so far away, on the refrigerator with magnets. look at their smiling faces as you remind yourself to eat. if you don't, then you will become weaker, and it will become harder, to live a life alone. after all, you only have your own strength to rely on. when you've had a particularly bad day, make yourself a lobster tail sandwich. learn how to warm the butter up just right, so it doesn't melt the mayonnaise. feel accomplished, and grown up, and decide the frozen lobster from the grocery store is a luxury you deserve. think about how much more expensive it would be if you had to share it with someone. laugh about being alone. feel your lungs expanding, your face taking in the sunlight, how nice it feels to poke fun at your situation from time to time. worry about schoolwork, and deadlines. annoy your online friends with your worries, and your to-do lists, and apologize, when you can, for being too much, because someone once taught you that you're hard to love. or did you convince yourself of that. answer the phone on the first ring when your mom calls, so she won't be scared that something happened to you, as if the twelve hours time difference between you means at the close of her eyelids, you could disappear, and she would have no way of knowing. tell your mom you miss her, and your dog, and let the tears fall, because it lets you feel loved for a second, and lets her feel needed. linger a minute more in the silence after you hang up with each other, the air sucking back out of your lungs, the chairs in the room empty again, the groceries in the fridge suddenly seeming too abundant. drive home after dance class and sink into your couch with exhaustion. struggle to find the motivation to make dinner, or take a shower. fall into the pillows and try not to fall asleep. drive yourself to the hospital when you're sick. hold your own hair back when you're throwing up in the bathroom, and a cold towel to your forehead. act like it's funny when your classmates call you kleenex girl, because you're so sick you bring a box of tissues to class every day, but stress over your grades so much, you can't afford to stay home. walk to the pharmacy down the street to pick up your own prescription, and cry at the counter when you realize you forgot your i.d., and you're going to have to walk home, and back again, your fever raging, your knees trembling. make enough chicken soup to last you a week. tell your online friends you're now a soup connoisseur, with lots of hahahas, so they won't notice how much you're struggling, so it won't feel like a big deal, when you're crying over the stove and all you want is to lay down. wish you had someone to take care of you. tell yourself no, you can take care of yourself. this is what people do. don't be weak. beat yourself up, constantly, for not measuring up, to how you view others living around you, to the dream you had grafted of how your life would be. go to the mall and walk the long promenades. peer into the store windows and think up little stories for each display, invent new lives for the mannequins, friends and family, jobs, and cozy houses. never imagine them being alone. notice how the world seems oblivious to your solitude, as if you are walking there as a completely separate entity, and no one sees, how you are alone. spend time thinking about the palm trees mingling overhead, present in every nook and corner of this island. spend the afternoon tangled up in the sway of their fronds, of the freedom to move through space with the wind, and yet still remain tethered in place. lie in your bed at night and think about how maybe being alone isn't so bad. think about how things wouldn't be better if you weren't here. back-pedal your thoughts from the other night, when you heard a creak in the floorboards, and you wondered if you were to die, how long would it take for someone to find you. would it be the smell, or the concern, that revealed your body. talk out loud to yourself in the dark of the room. tell yourself you're okay. that you're safe. spend some time noticing how small and hoarse your voice sounds, after not speaking out loud for three days. think of the auntie behind the cash register at the store, who was the last person you spoke to face to face, and how she complimented your glasses. wish you had said more than a quick thank you and fastened your eyes to the floor. think of your faraway friends. of the timezones, and continents, and borders, pushing you each into different corners of the world, and yet above it all, see your hands, clasped together, across the distances, arms like beanstalks stretching over the clouds. feel the weight of their supportive replies and the memories you share. put aside your phone and stare at the door. see your foot there, perched over the threshold, your other foot still within the room. pull at your legs to bring them both in, to bring them close. grow tired of not being there, and yet not being here. wish to stop wishing you were always someplace else. when here is where you wished to be, and now there is all you think of. remember the pua melia. wafting from the trees like ethereal parcels, a kaleidoscope of warm scents, signaling that it's okay, if this is home, if this is being alone.

And my son said
By Nicola Neal

Stop trying so hard
Just because you can't be a writer today
doesn't mean you won't be one day
Don't give up
Don't over think it
It can be about anything
Look in the fridge
It could be one of my yogurts.

The Chickpea
By Rosemarie Dillon

You're eating dinner when the cramps start. The tugging ache causes your smile to twist into a grimace. Your half-eaten quesadilla lays abandoned as you press your nails into your palm. *This is normal.*

Once the bleeding starts, you go to a movie. The theater popcorn you'd been looking forward to turns to a buttery sludge in your mouth. *A lot of people bleed in the beginning.* You'd be lying if you said you paid much attention to the movie.

The pain has gotten worse by the time you see the doctor. Framed by the dishwater gray sky behind the murky window, the doctor tells you that the test has come back negative. They tell you to prepare yourself for the inevitable, handing you a pamphlet. They tell you to call the office once you've passed the tissue to schedule more hormone injections, as if your world hadn't just imploded. *Maybe they're wrong.*

You become a prisoner of your bedroom for the next few days, staring at the red plastic container across the room filled with discarded needles. The pain has reduced you to a wet pile of putty. You try to avoid the restroom, but nature demands attention. As the blood sloughs out of you, something dense, no bigger than a chickpea, sits cradled amongst the carnage of the tissue.

Icy dread rolls down your body in a thick slime. Without another thought, you pluck the mass from the glob of uterine lining and wrap it in clean tissue. You place the small mound by your bedside and sink back into the mattress. Your eyes never blink, focusing on the scarlet blooming on the two-ply.

A warm hand squeezes your shoulder, and a glass of water appears in your eyeline, altering your perception. You drink, the grumble in your stomach sternly reminding you that you have not eaten since the sodden popcorn. Your eyes fall back to the balled-up tissue on your side table. The ache in your heart dwarfs any hunger pains you may have had.

You wake up in the hospital, a needle pumping fluid into your arm. A nurse threatens to admit you to the psych ward if you don't eat. Someone pats your hand and a bowl of soup slides into your view on the table before you. It isn't that you were not eating purposefully, you had merely not been hungry. After the soup has been dutifully ingested and the IV has dripped, you are released.

You move the chickpea to a crushed velvet necklace box when you get home and place it in a drawer. You glance up at a mirror to your immediate right and the reaper stares back at you. You see a wretched monster. A murderer of babies. You dig your nails into your forearms until they are stained crimson. An angry hand yanks your nails away from the bleeding flesh. Your arm is patched in silent rage, the door slamming afterwards.

You bleed for a month. The time comes when the world insists on your return. Work is to be done. Your bank account demands funding. Co-workers greet you jovially, asking how your vacation was.

Fantastic, Betty! My body murdered my baby. How have you been?

You somehow muster a hollow smile to assuage them. You guard the secret of your chickpea and are not quite sure why. To your great relief, work keeps you busy, until you catch the murderer's reflection in the shiny surface of your desk. You find your nails have buried themselves into the tender flesh of your arm yet again. You tug your shirt sleeve down to cover the bloody crescents.

Weeks pass in the same fashion. Hollow smiles. Work. Red waning moons. Repeat. You come home to an empty house each night. You are aware someone important used to share the space with you. The foggy memory of an argument, crying, and the packing of bags climbs into your mind. No longer will a large warm palm comfort you and give you glasses of water.

It's just you and the chickpea.

Your frozen dinner has been blasted by the microwave, a large glass of wine sits before you, and silence pulls up a chair to join you at the table. The chickpea remains in its box in your drawer. You swallow the food without tasting, drink the wine, and cry yourself to sleep on the couch with sharp fingernails hooking into your arm meat.

You've taken to wearing long sleeves at work, even in the sweltering August heat. You claim the air conditioner blows directly on you. You don't consider the moons as self-harm, after all, it isn't as if they will leave a scar.

After excessive needling from your co-workers, you find yourself at happy hour instead of eating dinner with silence. You may have overindulged as your head is a bit warbly and a lazy grin has plastered itself on your face. Your co-workers decide to bar hop after a round of lemon drop shots. It occurs to you that this is the first time since the chickpea that you have had a glimmer of happiness fill your heart.

Susan From Marketing gasps and all heads swivel in her direction. She is jumping up and down beside the smiling Chelsea From Accounting. Chelsea From Accounting announces she is twelve weeks pregnant. There is a collective shriek through the group while the floor falls out beneath your feet. What little happiness had begun to sprout in the darkness was stomped on by Chelsea's kitten heels. It is as if the sink holding all your feelings is suddenly uncorked, emotions flooding through the drain. You can see a couple of faces turn your way as tears spring to your eyes and blur your vision. Your chest tightens, heart hammering, and you step backward into the street. You swear you didn't see the car before it hit you.

But maybe you did.

The hospital lights sear your corneas as you wake. You can see your left leg encased in a cast, suspended in the air by a pulley system. You can't move your arms and your neck is being held still. A man with a full red beard touches your hand and rushes out of the room. Your eyes are still adjusting to the light when the bearded man returns with a doctor. She smiles sweetly at you and asks the man to step out. He looks crestfallen as he locks eyes with you. You realize now, this is your husband. The same man who left you in your time of anguish. You don't remember him having a beard when he left. He shuts the door behind him with a soft click and the doctor pulls up a chair beside you.

"You were hit by an SUV," she says, "You were very lucky."

You haven't the heart to tell her how wrong she is.

"I wanted to ask," she taps her clipboard with her pen, "Were you recently pregnant?" Ice runs through your veins.

"Yes. Ended in miscarriage," you whisper. This is the first time you've said the words aloud. They taste like vinegar in your mouth.

"Ah. I'm very sorry for your loss," she gently touches your non-broken leg in sympathy. The doctor's eyes slide over your exposed arms, no doubt noticing the crescents. "It may give you some small comfort to know that we found fetal cells at the sights of your wounds. This sometimes happens after miscarriage or birth. It's called Fetal Microchimerism. When a mother's experienced trauma after a pregnancy, the fetal cells in the blood rush to the sight of trauma. The cells can help repair damaged tissue by forming new blood vessels. You nearly bled out," she paused, "So what I'm trying to tell you, is that your baby helped to save your life." The doctor's words fade into the beeping of the machines. Big lumpy tears blur your vision as the realization hits you. A part of your baby will live in the same body that killed it, for years, according to the doctor. You ask to see your husband now. The doctor nods and pats your fingers again. "I'll send a psychiatrist down to speak with you," she says before exiting. You quietly thank her.

Your husband returns seconds after the doctor leaves and sits in your eyeline. He apologizes for leaving. He sobs into his hands and apologizes until his voice runs out. You grip his arm, and he looks up at you.

"You were grieving too. I'm sorry for not understanding," you whisper. He presses his forehead against yours, unable to wrap your broken body in an embrace.

"We're partners. I should never have left you to carry this alone."

You close your eyes and allow the solace to engulf you. You both understand the healing will take time and work, but a piece of your baby will live on inside of you.

And that will have to suffice.

Contributors:

Cover Artist:

Karen Boissonneault-Gauthier is an Indigenous photographer and writer. Most recently she's been nominated for Best on the Net. She's been a cover artist for *The Unmooring, Dyst, Synkroniciti, The Pine Cone Review, The Feeel Magazine, Arachne Press, Pretty Owl Poetry, Wild Musette, Existere Journal, Vine Leaves Literary Journal, Gigantic Sequins, Ottawa Arts Journal* and many more. She's been featured in Bracken, Vox Popular Media Arts Festival, Zoetic Press, New Feathers Anthology, Maintenant 15, Parliament Lit, Pure in Heart Stories and others. See www.kcbgphoto.com to find out more.

Marie-Andree Auclair's poems have found homes in many print and online publications in Canada, the USA, UK, Ireland, and Australia, most recently in Bywords (Canada); *Flo Lit Magazine* (Canada); *Young Ravens Review* (USA); and forthcoming in *Blue Lake Review* (USA). She lives in Canada.

Jerrice J. Baptiste is a published author of seven children's books and one adult poetry book *Wintry Mix*. The founder of Authentic Poetry workshops in The Hudson Valley for eighteen years, she has facilitated poetry as the Poet-in-Residence at The Prattsville Art Center & Residency since 2021. Her poetry has been included in the

Poetic License—Exhibitions at The Arts Society of Kingston (ASK), and in many reputable journals & magazines. She has been nominated as Best of The Net for 2022 by *Blue Stem*. Jerrice has been the featured poet on Planet Poet-Words in Space, The Woodstock Poetry Society, and The International Women's Writing Guild. Her poetry and collaborative song-writing are on the Grammy award nominated album- Many Hands: Family Music for Haiti.

Allison Collins is editor of *Upstate Life Magazine* and a writer with *The Daily Star* and *Kaatskill Life Magazine*. Her poetry and fiction have been published in online and print journals. Allison lives in upstate New York with her family.

Jennie Dear is the author of *What Does it Feel Like to Die?*, a nonfiction book about what researchers, palliative care experts, and dying patients know about the experience. (You can find relevant articles she's written at https://www.theatlantic.com/author/jennie-dear/). She's currently working on a combination of short stories, a book about where old people live, and a *Substack* essay series on the poetry and poignancy of dementia: https://jenniedear.substack.com.

K. Degala-Paraíso (she/they) is a Filipinx-American experimental writer living in Los Angeles. Her work has appeared in *miniskirt magazine, [PANK] Magazine, Okay Donkey Magazine,* and elsewhere; and has been nominated for a Pushcart Prize. She teaches creative writing through GrubStreet. She loves key lime pie dearly. Follow K. at kdegalaparaiso.com.

Rosemarie Dillon lives in New York with her family. When she isn't working her nine to five, she's writing in her closet office, reading under her pile of children, or actively keeping her toddler from jumping off the highest ledge he can find. She has written and illustrated two children's books with adult novels in the works. To stay updated on Rosemarie's current projects, visit her website https://www.rosemariedillon.com/.

Dion Farquhar has recent poems in *Non-Binary Review, Superpresent, Blind Field, Poesis, Cape Rock: Poetry, Poydras Review, Mortar, Local Nomad, Columbia Poetry Review, moria, Shifter, BlazeVOX*, etc. Her third poetry book *Don't Bother* is in press at Finishing Line Press, and she has three chapbooks. She works as an exploited adjunct at two universities, but still loves the classroom, and she is active in the University of California Santa Cruz adjunct union, the UC-AFT.

Erika B. Girard is currently pursuing her M.A. in English and Creative Writing with a concentration in Poetry through SNHU. Originally from Rhode Island, she derives creative inspiration from her family, friends, faith, and fascination with the human experience. She is a proofreader for *Wild Roof Journal*, an online literary journal with issues published bimonthly. Her own creative work appears or is forthcoming in *The Alembic, Iris Literary Journal, Untenured, Viewless Wings,* and more.

Sarah Grace Goolden (she/her) is in the throes of writing her Creative Writing MFA thesis at American University. She serves as the Poetry Editor for *FOLIO Magazine*. Sarah Grace is a graduate of University of North Carolina Greensboro & a former high school English teacher. Her poetry can be found in *The Appalachian Review, Dead Skunk Magazine, The Dillydoun Review & The Coraddi* & her journalism appears in *The Carolinian*, where she served as the Opinions Editor for four years. Sarah Grace is currently a bookseller, as well as a cat & rat mom.

Maxwell Griego is currently pursuing his MFA and writing whatever poetry comes to him along the way. He tends to be influenced by the nature around him, the soft & quiet moments in life, and his experiences as a queer man.

Taylor Leigh Harper is a Filipino American writer living in Southern California. Her writing has appeared in *LEON Literary Review, Rougarou, The Ilanot Review, SPLASH!, In Parentheses*, and elsewhere. She is a contributing writer and curator for agoodmovietowatch. When she is not writing, you can find her on Twitter @misstaywrites or Instagram @misstayleigh.

Vivian Holland lives in Brooklyn. She is in what can be considered a polyamorous relationship with writing, chemistry, and jazz. Her work has been published by or is forthcoming in *Bullshit Lit, LIGEIA, Autofocus* and elsewhere. You can read more at vivianholland.com or @VivWritesStuff on Twitter.

Zachary Kluckman is an award-winning poet who has been recognized for his performance, writing, and mentorship in poetry. With numerous poems appearing in print worldwide, as well as many appearances across the country, Kluckman was ranked as the fifth top slam poet in the nation at the Blackberry Peach National Poetry Slam. His work has been featured online in multiple formats. He is the author of the poetry collections, *The Animals in Our Flesh* (Red Mountain Press, 2012), *Some of It is Muscle* (Swimming with Elephants Publications, LLC, 2013) and the forthcoming *Rearview Funhouse* (Eyewear Publishing, 2022) You can find him on Instagram @physicalpoet.

Sasha Leshner is a writer living in New York. Her work draws on the dynamics of language, memory, and the impulses of our articulations. She has an MFA in Poetry from Columbia University and a BA from NYU. Her work has been published in *The*

Quarterless Review, ExPat Press, 89+ and the *luma foundation*, among others. She has written in collaboration with artists and organizations such as IM Studios and poet Richard Kostelanetz, and has worked as an editor at *The Columbia Journal, west 10th magazine, Gigantic Magazine,* and elsewhere. Her poems are dedicated to the beloveds who beat her to the next world.

Isabel Mader is a poet and essayist, as well as a parent and teacher. She holds an MFA from Fairleigh Dickinson University; the hood hangs next to her raincoat. Her poems were recently included in *Clockhouse Literary Journal* and *Slipstream Magazine.* Her latest essay can be found at *Insider Magazine.* She is most often found on the playground with her two children.

Darlene Montonaro is a poet from Cleveland, Ohio, whose work has appeared in *Calyx, Slipstream, The Raven Review, Earth's Daughters, Blueline, The Comstock Review,* and *The Buddhist Poetry Review* among other journals. She was the recipient of a 2016 writing fellowship from Community Partnership for Arts & Culture, and currently teaches creative writing at Literary Cleveland.

Nicola Neal is a 49-year-old writer from Bedfordshire, England. She started her writing career in journalism, before moving into copywriting. She recently completed an MA in Creative Writing at the University of Hertfordshire and since then has been working on developing her poetry and short story writing portfolio.

David Park is a retired educator / interpreter who was raised in small towns in western Pennsylvania and the Hudson River Valley. He went on to spend his adult life in San Francisco, Erie, Seattle, and Peru. In all of those places he has been made aware of the power and beauty of the written and spoken word, whatever the language.

Christian Paulisich is an undergraduate poet at Johns Hopkins University. He lives in Baltimore, Maryland, but is originally from the Bay Area, California. His poems have appeared or are forthcoming in *The Ocotillo Review, Pangyrus, Rust and Moth, The Concrete Desert Review, Twenty-two Twenty-eight, Invisible City, As It Ought to Be, Orchards Poetry Journal, Beltway Poetry Quarterly, Neologism Poetry Journal* and others.

Lexie Price is a 23-year-old poet currently based out of Arkansas. A University of Arkansas graduate, she considers writing her best tool for trying to make sense of a world not easily made sense of. Many of her poems focus on themes of dissociation, alienation, and the complexity of human nature. She has a special affinity for em dashes and the musicality of wordplay.

Charissa Roberson is a young writer and life-long reader from Lake Linganore, Maryland. She recently earned her bachelor's degree from Roanoke College, where she studied creative writing, French, and film. Her poetry and prose have appeared in several places in print and online, including *Running Wild Anthology of Stories* Vol. 6, *River and South Review, 45th Parallel, Burnt Pine Magazine, Elevation Review*, and *Manawaker Studio's Flash Fiction Podcast*. When not dwelling in imaginary worlds of words, she loves exploring the real one, watching and making films, learning languages, and playing Irish tunes on her fiddle.

Christina Roscoe is a public interest attorney and, most recently, an elementary school Teacher's Assistant. She and her wife live in New York. They have two children and two cats. In her free time, Christina writes, landscapes, and drinks large quantities of mediocre coffee. You can read more of her work in the Fall 2022 issue of *3Elements Literary Review* (No. 36) ("Enough for Both of Us" (Pushcart-nominated)). To the other new writers out there: it only takes one "yes." Keep submitting!

Kira Santana (she/her) currently lives on the island of Oʻahu, where she is a graduate student, poet, and hula dancer. Her work is deeply influenced by her experiences with chronic illness, and her childhood growing up in Norway. Kristin received the 2019 Myrle Clark Award for Creative Writing, in 2022, she was given the Hemingway Award, and in 2020, she was honored for her work in

Creative Writing at the University of Hawai'i's undergraduate showcase "English Represents!"

Kay Smith-Blum, a recovering retailer and former President of the Seattle School Board, has written two novels of historical fiction, currently out for small press review. Essays from her "Virus Days" humor series, nominated for Best of the Net 2020, are published in *Heavy Feather Review, Pif Magazine, The Furious Gazelle* and several other fine journals." Her short piece, "On Edge," was nominated for a 2023 Pushcart Prize. Smith-Blum's short works can be found now or in the future at *Fiction Southeast, Yellow Arrow Journal, Adelaide Magazine, Minerva Rising* and many more.

Ingrid L. Taylor is a poet, essayist, and veterinarian whose work has most recently appeared in the *Southwest Review, Red Canary Magazine, Collateral Journal*, and others. She has received *Punt Volat Journal's* Annual Poetry Award, is a Pushcart nominee, and was a featured poet in the *Horror Writers Association's Annual Poetry Showcase*, vol. 8. Her nonfiction has appeared in *HuffPost, Sentient Media, Feminist Food Journal,* and others. She has been awarded support for her writing from the Playa Artist Residency, the Horror Writers Association, and Gemini Ink. Find out more about her work at ingridltaylorwrites.com.

Rachel Azona Warshaw is a recent graduate of Macalester College. She is currently a staff member of *hu the zine*, a Florida-based arts magazine. Her poetry has appeared and is forthcoming in the *Denver Quarterly, Angel City Review, QA Poetry, Chanter Literary Magazine,* and *Mercury Zine*. Her short plays have been performed by various theatres in Seattle. After many winters in Minnesota, San Francisco is now her home base, where she waits upon a baby (professionally) and two cats (blood oath).

Cloe Watson is a graduate of the MFA program at Bowling Green State University. Her work has been featured in *Cimarron Review, Atlas and Alice, Flying Island Literary Journal, Blue Unicorn, The Windsor Review, Oakland Review, Grand Little Things, The Racket Journal, Wingless Dreamer, Beyond Words Literary Magazine* and *Defunkt Magazine*.

Haley Wilson is currently living in Virginia and working in national dropout recovery. After several years as a student and teacher of English Literature, writing is her passion project. She can typically be found writing by moonlight or sunrise along the Atlantic shore.

Alisha Wong is a writer and college freshman from the Midwest. Her writing has been recognized by the Alliance for Young Artists and Writers, St. Mary's College, and the Ledbury Poetry Festival, among others. Her other works are found or forthcoming in

UChicago's Euphony Journal, The Rising Phoenix Review, Up North Lit, and *Polyphony Lit*. In her spare time, she enjoys calligraphy, fashion, and black coffee.

Sophia Zhao is from Newark, Delaware. Her paintings and poetry appear in *The Adroit Journal, Up the Staircase Quarterly, The Indianapolis Review, The Minnesota Review,* and elsewhere. She currently studies at Yale University.

We love seeing photos of readers enjoying *Black Fox*! Be sure to tag us in your social media posts!

Thank you for reading! Stay in touch:

www.blackfoxlitmag.com
Website

www.facebook.com/blackfoxlit
Facebook

@blackfoxlit
Twitter & Instagram

www.blackfoxlitmag.com/contact/
Newsletter

Check out some of our previous issues:

Resources for Writers from BFLM Editor Racquel Henry's Writer's Atelier:

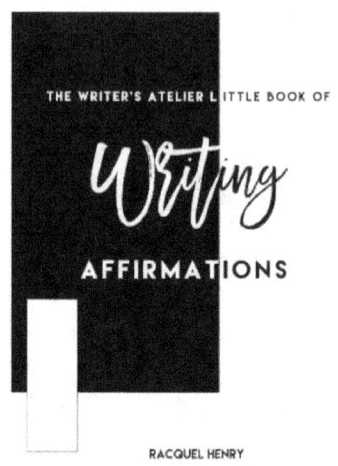

The Writer's Atelier Little Book of Writing Affirmations

The Write Gym Workbook by Racquel Henry

Join Racquel's free online community for writers:

writersatelier.mn.co